VOICES AT WHISPER BEND

❧

by
Katherine Ayres

American Girl™

Published by Pleasant Company Publications
© Copyright 1999 by Pleasant Company
All rights reserved.
For information, address: Book Editor, Pleasant Company Publications,
8400 Fairway Place, P.O. Box 620998, Middleton, WI 53562.

Printed in the United States of America.
99 00 01 02 03 04 RRD 10 9 8 7 6 5 4 3 2 1

History Mysteries™ and American Girl™
are trademarks of Pleasant Company.

PICTURE CREDITS
The following individuals and organizations have generously given permission
to reprint illustrations contained in "A Peek into the Past": p. 157—©Corbis; pp. 158-159—
©Corbis/Bettman-UPI (Roosevelt); *J and L's* by Theodore Allmendinger, courtesy Greater Latrobe
(PA) Senior High School (factory); Franklin D. Roosevelt Library, #NLR-PHOCO-65702(40) (girl);
pp. 160-161—Library of Congress, #LC-USW3-9700-D (scrap pile); Culver Pictures (poster);
©Corbis/Bettman-UPI (grocery); State Historical Society of Wisconsin, neg. #(X3)52130 (ration
coupons); Franklin D. Roosevelt Library (worker); Popperfoto/Archive Photos (air-raid shelter); pp.
162-163—from the book *Victory at Sea* by Richard Hanser (ship); National Archives, #111-SC-345-
140 (mail call); Blethen Maine Newspapers, Inc. (children); p. 165—Bill Sauers Photo.

Cover and Map Illustrations: Dahl Taylor
Line Art: Greg Dearth
Editor: Peg Ross
Art Direction: Jane Varda
Design: Laura Moberly and Kim Strother

Library of Congress Cataloging-in-Publication Data

Ayers, Katherine.
Voices at Whisper Bend / by Katherine Ayers. — 1st ed.
p. cm. — (History mysteries)
"American girl."
Summary: In their Pennsylvania town in 1942 twelve-year-old Charlotte
and her classmates collect scrap metal for the war effort only to have it disappear
from the school basement.

ISBN 1-56247-817-6 (alk. paper). ISBN 1-56247-761-7 (pbk. : alk. paper)
1. World War, 1939-1945 — Pennsylvania Juvenile fiction.
[1. World War, 1939-1945—United States Fiction. 2. Pennsylvania Fiction.
3. Mystery and detective stories.]
I. American girl (Middleton, Wis.) II. Title. III. Series.
PZ7.A9856Vo 1999 [Fic]—dc21 99-24456 CIP

for Elena, for Rachel
my daughters, my friends

TABLE OF CONTENTS

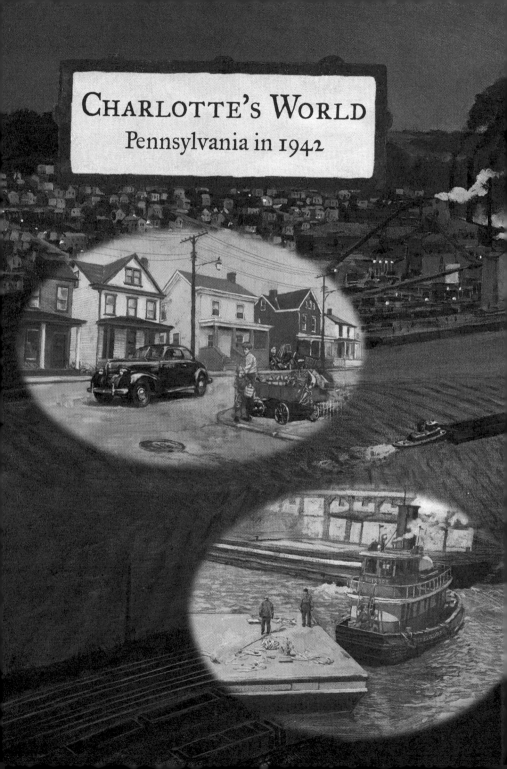

CHARLOTTE'S WORLD
Pennsylvania in 1942

CHAPTER I

BOATS

 How was school, honey? Did you do all right on that history quiz?" Ma stood at the kitchen sink, peeling vegetables for homemade soup.

"The quiz was postponed," Charlotte began. "We had—"

"We had an air-raid drill," Robbie interrupted. "A long, scary one. And I got stuck sitting between two girls. Phewie!" He waved his hand in front of his nose.

Charlotte pushed back from the kitchen table where she was mixing black, blue, and white paints in a can. "You stop that right now, Robbie Campbell, or I won't paint your dumb tugboat for you."

"But, Charlie, you promised," Robbie protested.

"Spit on your hand and swear then, buster," Charlotte said. "Repeat after me. Girls do not stink."

Robbie raised a grubby hand, palm facing toward her. "Some girls do not stink. Is that good enough?"

He wrinkled his nose and Charlotte held back a laugh.

"Why don't you quit while you're ahead, Robbie?" Ma said with a grin. She turned to look at Charlotte. "Was the drill a bad one?"

Charlotte shrugged. She swirled the paint in the can with a wooden stick, making the white disappear into the darker colors. "Like Robbie said, it took a long time."

"Did many kids get upset this time? Did Betsy?" Ma wore her serious look. Betsy Schmidt lived next door. She and Charlotte had been best friends forever. So had their mothers.

Charlotte didn't want to be disloyal to her friend, but she couldn't lie, either. "Betsy cried some. So did a few other kids. The Cussick twins always pray during the drills. I know that should make me feel better, but instead I feel worse. Like we're really in trouble and it's not just practice."

"I wish we lived out in the country," Robbie said. "Even those mean old Germans wouldn't bomb cows."

"I'm sure they don't plan on bombing schoolchildren, either," Ma said. She sat between Charlotte and Robbie at the table and took their hands in hers. "You both know it's a precaution, don't you? The school turns out the lights just in case—so it won't look like a war factory from above and become a target like the steel mills are. But you're not to worry. German warplanes haven't crossed the Atlantic Ocean yet, and we pray they never do."

Charlotte nodded. But sometimes it was hard not to worry. In a factory town like Braddock, the air-raid drills came once a month, with blaring sirens, and quite a few kids got upset. Teachers postponed tests and homework afterward.

"I'm glad Pa works on the *Rose*," Robbie said. "If he sees a German warplane, or even hears one, he'll rev up his engines and zoom away so fast his wake will smack the shore like ocean waves. *Vroom!*" Robbie lifted his home-made wooden tugboat and put her through maneuvers that would capsize the biggest tug on the river. "I guess we're luckier than Betsy, aren't we?"

Ma nodded. She didn't say the words, but Charlotte knew what she was thinking. Betsy's father worked at the Edgar Thomson, the steel mill upriver. Now *that* was a target. Huge brick chimneys soared into the sky, blowing out smoke and shooting flames all day and all night. They could never douse the lights of the steel mill, nor hide those tall chimneys from a bomber. All along the Monongahela River from Pittsburgh to West Virginia, mills were belching out smoke and flame, proud to be helping the war. Targets, every one of them.

Robbie nudged Charlotte's arm. He sailed his tug right under her nose. "Are you going to mix all day, or are you going to paint?"

Ma smiled again, and returned to her vegetables.

Charlotte shook her head. Were all nine-year-olds so

impatient? "Hand it over. Is this color close enough to the *Rose?*" She daubed the stirring stick on the newspaper that covered the kitchen table.

"Not bad, for a girl."

"I'll paint *you* if you don't watch out." She took the boat from him and waved a dry brush at his right cheek.

The color she'd concocted pleased her. The main deck, hull, and engine room of Pa's tug were the same dark blue-gray she'd mixed. The engine house rose up high above it, a scrubbed, clean white. And Pa had chosen bright blue for the stacks. Robbie had done a pretty good job with the model. Of course, he'd had help. Their older brother Jim had taught him how to use the chisel and plane and how to get the size right.

"I want to make barges too, Charlie, but I can't figure out what wood to use. Everything we've got is too thick. And with Jim gone and Pa so busy, I don't have anyone to help me with the saw."

"I know." Charlotte dipped her brush and began to smooth paint on the wooden hull. She kept her eyes focused on the brush and the pine boat. She didn't want to look at Ma's back, which was sure to be stiff at the mention of Jim. "How about an orange crate? Bet you could find an empty one at the market. Those boards are real thin. You'd just have to watch out for splinters."

"I got sandpaper. I'm a good sander. And I could paint rocks black and glue them on the barge, for coal." He stood. "Can I go now, Ma? Can I try the market?"

"Isn't it still raining?" Ma asked. She lifted one of the kitchen curtains aside.

"Just April showers. I won't melt. Please, Ma?" He was hopping up and down on one foot.

Ma nodded. "Okay. But just to the market and right back. No sightseeing today, mister. And dry your feet when you get home."

Robbie dashed out the back door. Charlotte continued to paint. She felt Ma's hand on her shoulder. "It's nice of you to help your brother with his boats."

"This size boat I can handle," Charlotte said.

Ma nodded, a faraway look in her eye. "He misses Jim a lot."

"He's not the only one, Ma," Charlotte said. She set down the paintbrush and boat, stood and leaned into Ma's shoulder. "Where do you suppose he is right now?"

"God only knows," Ma said, scrubbing hard at a carrot. "God and the admirals."

Later that evening, Charlotte sat close to the radio and listened hard to the President's voice as he told the country bad news. Robbie lay on his stomach on the carpet next to her and rested his chin in his hands. As usual, his dark hair stuck up in messy tufts. Across the room, Ma sat close to

Pa on the sofa, still wearing her apron. She stared at the
radio as if Mr. Franklin Delano Roosevelt himself were
going to step out of that wooden case and sit down on the
green rocking chair where Jim used to sit, to tell them
how badly the war was going.

Charlotte traced the large tan roses in the carpet as
the President's crackling voice reviewed all the battles lost
to Germany and Japan. Then his voice softened, and she
listened harder.

*"As we here at home contemplate our own duties, our own
responsibilities, let us think and think hard of the example which
is being set for us by our fighting men."*

They're on my mind all the time, Charlotte answered
him silently.

The President continued. *"Our soldiers and sailors are . . ."*

They're our brothers, Charlotte thought, like Jim. Back
in December when America joined the war, he'd gone in
and talked to Mr. Butler at the draft board. Mr. Butler had
suggested that Jim would make a swell sailor, what with
helping on Pa's tug most of his life. So Jim had enlisted in
the Navy and traded the Monongahela River for an ocean
somewhere.

Charlotte blinked and turned toward Ma for comfort,
but Ma's eyes looked swimmy. Next to Ma, Pa sat with his
hands clenched into fists.

The President's words brought pictures to Charlotte's
mind, pictures from the newsreels. She'd seen the map of

France covered by a big black swastika. Seen the long lines
of German soldiers marching in their heavy black boots.
Seen a huge ship take a hit from a torpedo and roll over
into the ocean, dumping all the sailors overboard to die.

Mr. Roosevelt's fighting men were boys—brothers and
sons, cousins and neighbors.

*"They are the United States of America. That is why they
fight. We too are the United States of America. That is why we
must work and sacrifice.*

"It is for them. It is for us. It is for victory."

On the radio, a band began to play. Robbie stood up
and saluted the President. Pa switched off the set.

Ma straightened. Charlotte watched her blink a couple
of times, like she had a speck of dirt in her eye. Then she
cleared her throat and turned to Charlotte and Robbie.
"Your schoolwork done?"

"Yes, ma'am. But I got sanding and gluing to do."
Robbie saluted again and marched off to the kitchen and
his model boats.

"What about you, Charlotte?"

"Yes, Ma. There wasn't much schoolwork because of
that air-raid drill." Charlotte could tell that Ma wasn't really
worried about science or arithmetic—she just didn't want
to think about the war anymore.

"Then how about a game of dominoes, Lottie?" Pa
asked Charlotte. He rolled up the sleeves of his plaid shirt,
like he was ready for serious business.

Charlotte got out the wooden box of dominoes and took a seat on the floor next to a flat-topped trunk. Pa gathered pencil and paper from the lamp table and sat across from her.

As they turned the dominoes face-down and mixed them, Charlotte was still running the President's words over in her mind. He hadn't just talked about faraway battles; he'd spoken about people here at home, too. How they had to help the soldiers and sailors win the war. She spoke to Pa softly, so as not to bother Ma, who had pulled out her sewing basket and was threading a needle. "Mr. Roosevelt was talking about us tonight, Pa. How we all have to work hard and sacrifice."

"Yep, that he was."

"But, Pa, I don't understand. How can we help?"

Pa smiled at her. "Folks around here are already doing what they can. The mills are running night and day."

"I know," Charlotte sighed.

"And not just in Braddock," Pa said. "Up and down the Mon valley, we're pouring more steel every day. Makes a person proud."

"I know, Pa," Charlotte said again. "You're doing a lot, too. Running extra trips on the river so the mill won't run out of coke and coal and ore." Charlotte glanced toward the sofa. "Even Ma, she's over there patching a dress so more cloth can go for uniforms, but . . ."

Pa took her chin in his hand. "What's bothering you, sweetheart?"

"What about me, Pa? Mr. Roosevelt said every man, woman, and child. I'm twelve. How can I help fight the war? Jim's doing so much . . ."

"You're already saving your money and buying defense stamps. And you've helped your ma plant a victory garden."

"That's not enough."

"Wait till summer comes. You'll be weeding and watering, you and your brother. And you can help Ma with the canning and pickling." Pa reached into the boneyard for his seven dominoes.

"I did that before we went to war, Pa. I want to do something real." Charlotte picked her dominoes and set them up, checking the faces.

Pa held up a domino and grinned. "Ah, I got double eights. Unless you got the nines . . ."

"No. You go first, Pa." Charlotte sighed again. The only double she had was the double zero. Nothing. And that's about how useful she felt.

Before she went upstairs to bed, Charlotte stood beside the front window and looked out. Just another damp April night. She touched each point of the blue cloth star that hung in the window. Jim's star. Ma had hung it up the day he left for the Navy, like every mother did who sent her son to war. But where was Jim now? How was he? Was it bedtime where he was, or morning? Dark or sunny?

With one finger, Charlotte planted a kiss on the top point of the star, just as she did every night at bedtime. "Good night, Jim. Wherever you are, sleep well."

Upstairs, Charlotte pulled on her nightgown, but she didn't feel sleepy. The President's words and the wail of the air-raid siren still echoed in her mind. She stood near the window and looked outside again, across the backyards. Upriver, the sky glowed orange-gold from the furnaces of the Edgar Thomson. Straight ahead, she could see a small piece of the Monongahela. With all the rain, the water would turn brown and muddy, and the current would pick up.

Charlotte shivered as she remembered another time when the river had run fast, filled with spring rains. Sometimes it felt like only yesterday, instead of years ago, when she'd run too fast along Pa's wet deck and slipped into the Mon. She couldn't forget how that oily brown water had closed over her head and she'd sunk down, down, into murky nothingness. When she'd tried to open her mouth to call for help, cold, choking water had rushed in, ripping like icy knives into her lungs. But Jim had been there to fish her out. He and Pa had pounded her chest and got her breathing again. She'd been all right after that, except when the memory came back in the middle of the night.

Nights like that, she missed Jim the most. He'd been there, he understood—she could knock on his door and he'd listen and then tell her stories until she felt all right again.

She hugged her arms, suddenly missing Jim with
a fierce, cold ache. Why did she still want to go cry
on her big brother's shoulder? After all, hadn't the
accident happened a long time ago? Hadn't she out-
grown all that?

As far as the rest of her family knew, she was fine.
And most of the time, she was. Most of the time, she
figured she was just a cat, a critter that didn't much like
the water. But a critter with nine lives. She'd used up
one of her nine that spring day when she was five and
slipped off the tug into the Mon.

Enough, Charlotte, she scolded herself. She'd be as
cranky as a cat if she didn't get to sleep soon. And there'd
be that postponed history quiz first thing in the morning.
A good grade would help her final report card. She
climbed into bed and pulled the blankets up to her chin.
Warm and dry, I'm warm and dry. Maybe if she said the
words often enough, she'd believe them. She closed her
eyes and waited for sleep.

In the night a dream came.

Charlotte sat up in bed, wide-awake and sweating as
bits of the dream still clung to her mind. There she was
in rough water, huge waves swelling and sinking all around.
Through the darkness, she could see Jim balancing near a

ship's rail. Then a lurch and a wash of seawater and Jim disappearing.

"Just a dream, a nightmare," Charlotte whispered to herself. She wiped sweat from her face with a corner of the sheet and took a deep breath. But the palms of her hands still stung where she'd dug her fingernails in, trying to hold on to that phantom ship's rail, and trying without success to sight her older brother in the whirling black water.

CHAPTER 2

SCRAPPERS

The next morning Charlotte knelt in the damp grass, petting a pale gray cat. He was one of the dozens that belonged to old Mrs. Dubner, who lived next door in the corner house. The cat's fur was matted and rough with burrs. Charlotte pulled a couple out. "Looks like you had a bad night too, kitty," she said. "Hope you didn't have bad dreams."

"Hey Charlotte!" Betsy called from her doorway on the other side of Charlotte's house. Betsy hurried to the sidewalk, pulling on a sweater, her pale brown pigtails bouncing. "Sorry I'm late again. Why are you petting that nasty cat? He probably has fleas. He looks like he's been in a fight."

"He just needs a good brushing," Charlotte said. She stood and stepped carefully across a wide crack in the sidewalk. "Betsy, did your family listen to the President last night?"

"Sure. Everyone here at home's going to have to pitch in. I'm buying an extra war stamp this week. How about you?"

Charlotte shrugged. "Buying a measly war stamp doesn't seem like much. Not with what our brothers are doing." They turned off Talbott and headed north, toward Braddock Avenue. Once they crossed Braddock, the climb would start, but for now the hill still lay in shadows, waiting to burn their leg muscles.

"We could lie about our age and get jobs at the mill," Betsy suggested. She pulled her shoulders back. "We're both tall."

Charlotte laughed. "They'd never believe us."

"What about the Red Cross? They'd let us help."

"Rolling bandages? Little old ladies do that." Charlotte shook her head. She and Betsy crossed Braddock Avenue, passing by all the stores and businesses, and began the long uphill climb. "I wish we could do something interesting," she continued. "Like being spies."

"Are you kidding?" Betsy huffed as she spoke. She wasn't much of a climber.

"Come on, Bets. We could do it. Nobody would ever suspect a couple of kids. We could sneak places and overhear war secrets."

Betsy shoved her shoulder. "You're nuts, Charlotte Campbell. What war secrets are we going to hear in Braddock, Pennsylvania? Nope, unless your brother can smuggle us onto a Navy ship and slip us into Germany or

France, we're not going to hear anything more interesting than Mrs. Dubner swearing at her cats."

Charlotte felt the familiar burn in the back of her calf muscles and picked up speed. The best way to make your legs stop aching was to get to school fast. She kicked at a stone and sent it flying across the street. "Mrs. Dubner does swear a blue streak. I caught Robbie using some of those words on Monday. Now he owes me."

Betsy shook her head. "Ma says she's a disgrace to the neighborhood. If she'd just clean her yard and porch, she wouldn't have to holler. Those poor cats are always bumping into trash and knocking cans over."

"She's old, Bets. And there's so much junk, it would take a whole company of soldiers to clean her place." Something glinted on the sidewalk and Charlotte stooped to pick it up.

"What'd you find?"

"Nothing. Just a bottle cap." She drew back her arm, ready to pitch it, then stopped stock-still. "Hold on a minute. Look at this." She showed the cap to Betsy. "What's it made of?"

"I don't know. Steel? Tin, maybe. Why? What are you thinking up, Charlotte?"

Charlotte smiled. She tossed the bottle cap into the air and caught it. Then she polished its smooth silvery top on her skirt. "That's it. That's what we're going to do for the war."

"Pick up bottle caps? Why? So we can throw them at the wicked Germans? That's about as dumb as being spies."

Charlotte turned and pointed upriver toward North Braddock. Huge billows of black smoke drifted across the morning sky from the giant mill chimneys. "Look, Bets, they're making more steel every day. People are having scrap metal drives all over the country, so mills like the Edgar Thomson can melt down the old metal and pour new steel for ships and planes."

"Scrap metal. Sure, we could collect that—steel and tin and aluminum! Charlotte, you're a genius."

"We'll get our class to help. Mrs. Alexander will go for it. She's been making us write all those paragraphs about freedom and the USA." Charlotte speeded her stride again. Uphill, the early bell rang.

"Slow down," Betsy said. "You're always in such a hurry, Charlotte. We've got five minutes. This hill's a killer."

"Come on, I want to talk to Mrs. Alexander right away. Before school starts." Charlotte stuck the bottle cap into her skirt pocket. Maybe she was in a rush, but today she had a good reason.

"I'll hurry, but if I pass out on the sidewalk, you'd better pick me up." Betsy's cheeks were red and she was huffing and puffing.

Charlotte's lungs burned too, but they only had a block left to walk. "I'll tell you what we'll be picking up. Old wheels and bent pots."

"Sounds like work," Betsy said. "But down by the river it wouldn't be so bad. You see a lot of old junk there. 'Course, we'd have to be careful. The banks can be steep."

Steep and slippery. Charlotte shuddered. "I've got a better idea. We'll start our drive right in old Mrs. Dubner's backyard. Just you wait, Bets. We'll be the best scrappers in Braddock."

Charlotte placed her right hand over her heart and recited the Pledge of Allegiance. On mornings like this one, when the President had just given a speech, it seemed like everybody stood a little straighter and spoke a little louder. Even her teacher wore a dark blue suit that looked military. Charlotte held her shoulders back the way Jim had taught her to do once he joined up. She wished that the flag hanging over the blackboard was bigger, and less faded.

Then Mrs. Alexander nodded for them to sit down. She perched on the edge of her desk. "Class, may I have your attention, please? Before we begin this morning's current events reports, Charlotte Campbell would like to speak to all of you."

Heads turned. Charlotte's stomach did somersaults. She stood and cleared her throat. "Um, I guess you all heard the President last night. I'd like to do something for the war. Not just buy stamps. Betsy and I got an idea.

We could start a metal drive, right here in Braddock. What do you think?"

Her cheeks burned. She slipped into her seat, fiddling with the bottle cap. Around the room she heard whispers. What would they say? Would they do it? Amazingly, most of the class liked her idea.

Then Sophie Jaworski raised her hand. "But what about lockjaw, Mrs. Alexander? You can get it from rusty metal."

Charlotte rolled her eyes at Betsy. They both knew what really worried Sophie—getting dirty, or, heaven help her, breaking a fingernail.

"Good question, Sophie. We'll have to be very careful."

Paul Rossi wanted to collect everything—rags, rubber, and paper, as well as metal—but Mrs. Alexander didn't agree. "Let's save something for the seventh and eighth graders to work on. I'll speak to their teachers. Now, on to current events."

Several kids reported on the President's talk, which seemed odd to Charlotte. Every family in America listened, so why tell what people already knew?

Sophie Jaworski pulled her news from the fashion pages as usual. "Hemlines Go Up to Save Fabric for Our Soldiers." It was war news, but barely. That girl!

When it was Paul Rossi's turn, he got out a newspaper clipping and read the headline. "'Woman Found on Church Steps.' Did you see this?" he asked. "It was in the morning paper. They found a dead woman on the steps of

St. Stanislas Catholic Church in Pittsburgh. She was wearing her nightgown and wrapped in a torn blanket. Nobody knows who she is. Nuts, isn't it? I've heard of people falling asleep in church, but this one never woke up."

When he sat down, a lot of the boys were grinning. Some laughed out loud and Mrs. Alexander had to shush them. How dare they laugh? It made Charlotte want to cry. The poor woman, left there like nobody cared about her.

Charlotte scowled. That Paul Rossi, he was always digging up creepy stuff from the newspapers. Murders and bodies and escaped convicts. What kind of person enjoyed reading about such things? She wished he lived in a different state.

After current events, they planned the scrap drive. Mrs. Alexander spoke to other teachers at lunch. By the end of the day, Charlotte's idea had caught fire in the whole school. The principal visited her class and explained what each grade would do. "Thanks to Charlotte, the sixth grade will become scrappers," he said. "The seventh grade wants to run a newspaper drive and save some trees for building barracks. We'll store the metal and the papers in the school cellar. And the eighth graders will roll old tires to the riverbank, where they'll be loaded on a barge and sent to a factory to make new tires. Younger students in first through fifth grades will help their older brothers and sisters." He shook Charlotte's hand before he left.

‎᷐

Back at home, Charlotte changed out of school clothes and rushed to meet Betsy in front of old Mrs. Dubner's house. Junk littered the small front yard and the porch. The only thing that kept the trash from spilling into the Campbells' yard was the tall wooden fence Pa had built between the yards. If the old lady's house had ever been painted, you couldn't tell what color, for it had faded to a soft, peeling gray.

"You knock," Betsy said. "I'm too nervous. What if she says no?"

"I'll knock, but we'll both ask her. That way she can't say no." Charlotte knocked, and the old lady answered as a pair of cats wove themselves around her thin legs. She wore a long, baggy dress and what looked like men's socks and slippers.

"We're having a metal drive," Betsy began.

"It's for the war," Charlotte added. "We wondered if you had any old stuff you didn't need." She pointed toward a rusty wheel in the front yard. "We could haul it away for you if you wouldn't mind."

Mrs. Dubner bent to pick up a gray-and-white cat. She scratched its ears. A light wind blew raggedy strands of white hair into her wrinkled face. "You'd clean my yard for me? How much?"

"For free," Charlotte said. "We're collecting metal.

We'll haul off things from your house too, if you'd like."

"The yard and the house too? For nothing? If that ain't a bargain. Sure. You gals help yourselves to all the junk you want. Ain't nothing out here I need." She closed the door.

"Let's start in the front yard," Betsy suggested. "The whole street will look better once we clean that up."

Charlotte nodded. "Fine with me."

She borrowed Robbie's wagon. Betsy brought three bushel baskets from her house, and they set to work. By suppertime, they'd filled them with tin cans and dented pails. They'd even piled two tires on the sidewalk for the eighth graders to pick up.

"See you tomorrow," Betsy said. "I'm tired and starving."

Charlotte grinned. "You're not too clean, either. Good thing there's nobody around with a camera, or they'd blackmail us for sure. See you tomorrow."

Charlotte let herself in the back door and scrubbed her hands before supper. She could hardly wait to tell Ma and Pa about the scrap drive. But first she carried steaming bowls of beef stew to the kitchen table as Ma poured milk for everybody. Then the family sat, and Charlotte waited for Pa to say the blessing.

"Guess what," she said as they began to eat. "I'm helping with the war."

"The whole school is helping," Robbie interrupted. "And it was Charlie's idea. Not bad, for a sister."

Pa smiled as Charlotte explained.

Ma looked thoughtful. "I'm proud of you, Charlotte." She paused for a moment, straightened her napkin, then looked up at the family. "I want to do my part too. I'm considering going to work."

"Work?" The word stuck in Charlotte's throat.

"What? Where?" Pa asked.

Ma rubbed her chin with her knuckles. "At first I thought I'd go down to Pittsburgh, to the Heinz plant. They put out a call for workers, and I thought maybe I could make rations for the troops. Might even end up fixing meals for our Jim."

"Did you get a job, Ma?" Robbie asked. His eyes were round.

"Not at Heinz. I phoned up first. They aren't looking for cooks. Turns out they've converted half their plant to make plywood for airplane parts. Besides, the plant's a long ride from here. So I decided to stop at the mill here in Braddock and see if they could use me."

"The Edgar Thomson?" Pa asked. Charlotte could tell from the look on his face that he was as surprised as she was.

Ma nodded. "They're making plate steel. A lot of it goes into ships for our Navy. I said I could start Monday."

"Wow, swell, Ma," Robbie said. He saluted her and then Charlotte. "All hands! Now everybody's helping Jim win the war."

Ma's cheeks turned pink. "James, what do you think?" she asked Pa.

He turned a serious face toward her. "I've hardly had a chance to think. What would you be doing in that mill? A lot of those jobs are heavy work, Mary. And dangerous."

"They seem to think they could train me to operate a crane."

Pa didn't speak right away. When he did, it sounded like he was picking out each word. "If . . . if it's what you want . . . I'll be proud. Proud of both my gals." He smiled at Charlotte. "You collect the metal, and your ma here will turn it into battleships."

Ma cleared her throat. "One thing," she began. "I know you'll be busy in school, Charlotte. And now this metal drive. But I'll need you to help with the housework, start supper for the family, and watch Robbie, especially when your pa's on the boat."

"Sure, Ma," Charlotte said, but her tongue felt like lead. She needed to spend every free moment hunting scrap metal. How could she help win the war if she had to do Ma's jobs too?

CHAPTER 3
CONFETTI LETTER

"Seaman First Class, Robert Michael Campbell, reporting for duty, sir." Supper was over. Charlotte was washing dishes and trying to figure out how to collect as much scrap as she could before Ma started at the mill. Robbie saluted, then reached for the dish towel.

"Cut it out," Charlotte grumbled. "You're not in the Navy."

"Not yet," Robbie said. "But when I'm old enough, I'm going to be a sailor, same as Jim. On a battleship."

"Who says he's on a battleship?" Charlotte asked. She scrubbed at a sticky spot on a plate. "He might be on a destroyer, a patrol boat, convoy duty. We don't know. We don't even know which ocean they've sent him to."

"Wherever they sent him, I'm going too." Robbie stuck out his chin.

Charlotte knew she'd never win that argument. She

Robbie rushed inside and headed upstairs, but Charlotte stepped into the kitchen slowly. It didn't feel right, coming home to a locked-up house—it felt cold and empty. Charlotte shut the door and glanced around the quiet kitchen. Ma had left a note on the table. Charlotte leaned over and read it.

Dear Children,
Please finish all your schoolwork before going outside. My shift goes until four o'clock and I'll take a while to walk home, so don't expect me before four-thirty or five. Don't forget to change into play clothes.

Love,
Mother

Charlotte looked up as Robbie bounced back into the kitchen and headed for the door. "Schoolwork first," Charlotte told him.

"Aw, come on, Charlie," he grumbled. "I want to get more stuff from that cellar. Ma won't know if I do my arithmetic now or later."

"Schoolwork first," she repeated. "Orders from the first mate."

He frowned and his shoulders slumped. "Aye, aye."

"I'll help if you get stuck with your multiplication," Charlotte offered. "Do the easy ones while I work on current events. Then we'll go to Mrs. Dubner's."

Charlotte nudged Robbie into a kitchen chair, then seated herself and unfolded the newspaper to check the headlines. "Two Convoy Ships Sunk in Shipping Lanes off Florida Keys." "Destroyer Crippled by Bombs in North Atlantic." Bad news for the Navy, and that meant bad news for Jim. She tried to ignore the sick feeling in her stomach and turned to the inside pages. "Three Men Hold Up South Side Bank." Great. That was a Paul Rossi article. She didn't need to read it—he'd tell all about it tomorrow. "Sugar Rationing to Begin, Meat Will Soon Follow." She clipped the column. That was an article she could tell about without crying in front of her class.

She and Robbie finished their work and repacked their books. They changed quickly and headed next door for Betsy.

"The cellar again?" Betsy asked as they turned up the sidewalk toward Mrs. Dubner's. "I wish we could work outside today. That sun feels so good. Spring's really here."

Charlotte nodded. "Come on, troops. To the cellar, spring or not. All the outside trash is gone." Charlotte knocked on the back door, then led the way down the rickety steps and found the string that worked the bare lightbulb. A moldy, damp, earth smell filled her nose. Deep in the shadows, spiderwebs hung as thick as curtains.

"Clear the decks," Robbie warned. He grabbed a broom and attacked the spiderwebs, covering himself in sticky dust.

Charlotte pried open a door off to one side, revealing a little room packed to the ceiling with old newspapers.

Betsy peered over her shoulder. "Hey, my cousin Pete's in seventh grade," she said. "He and his friends could haul these papers away for their drive. Shall I go find him?"

"Good idea. There's plenty of metal over there for us." Charlotte pointed to where Robbie had swept away the spiderwebs. As Betsy left, the two of them started clearing out the corner.

"Here's a lunch pail. Nice one too, except the catch is busted." Robbie tossed it into a bushel basket.

"Hey, look at this," he said. "Did Mrs. Dubner ever have a kid?" He lifted out a bent and twisted frame with four wheels. The bottom and sides were in shreds, but once, a long time ago, it had been a baby buggy. Robbie shoved it along the cellar floor, but one of the wheels was stuck so it wouldn't roll. "Did she have a kid, Charlie, or did she use the buggy for one of her cats?"

Charlotte ran her hand along the cold handle of the baby buggy. Her right thumb caught on a rough spot where rust had eaten away at the metal. She shoved the buggy toward Robbie. "I don't know. Add it to the stack."

The idea of Mrs. Dubner being somebody's mother felt strange. For all of Charlotte's life, the woman had been the neighborhood's odd person. She wasn't actually loony, but close to it, with her ancient, baggy clothes and her untidy wisps of hair. Charlotte had never imagined her having children. Had Mrs. Dubner just picked up the old buggy on the street and brought it home?

Charlotte didn't have time to think about it. Betsy arrived with her cousin and three of his friends. The older boys kept up a loud parade from the cellar to their wagons and wheelbarrow waiting on the sidewalk. Funny, Charlotte thought. Old Mrs. Dubner was doing her part to win the war without planning it.

"Wow! Look, Charlie. Bones!" Robbie bent over a rusty washtub.

A shiver ran up Charlotte's spine. "Don't be ridiculous. April Fools' is over."

"I'm not fooling," he said. "Come see."

Charlotte stooped and peered into the washtub. Betsy stood behind her. "He's right, Charlotte, those do look like bones. Tiny ones."

"Bet it's from a cat," Robbie said. "She has so many she wouldn't miss one."

"More like a kitten, from the size of the skull," Charlotte said, pointing. A sour taste rose to her mouth. Sometimes when you looked for one thing, you found something else. Something you'd never want to find.

"I'll fill up the washtub with junk and take it outside," Robbie offered.

Charlotte suspected he'd save the kitten bones first and sneak them into his room. Fine. She'd stay away from his room.

"Okay," she said. "After that, how about we quit for the day?"

When Ma came home she didn't even look like herself; her cheeks were smudged and she wore dirty overalls and a cap. First thing, she filled the tub for a long soak. Then she lay on the sofa and called out instructions for warming up the supper she'd made the day before.

That evening, Charlotte felt like she'd been drafted to fight on the home front. The kitchen became her battlefield, the old creaky stove, her enemy. She did her best with the cooking, but as the week wore on, she scorched potatoes and left hamburgers raw in the middle.

The newspapers had warned that rationing would begin any day, so people rushed to the stores to stock up on supplies before rationing started. That week, Charlotte stood in line twice for sugar and could only buy five pounds.

Still, whenever she had a few spare minutes, she rushed next door to work on Mrs. Dubner's cellar. By Friday, Charlotte was nearly as tired as Ma.

Her tiredness slipped away when Mrs. Alexander made an announcement late on Friday afternoon. "Congratulations, boys and girls. In just one week, this class has filled a room in the school cellar with metal. On Monday afternoon, a truck will come. All of you sixth graders are invited to stay after school to load the truck. Then we'll follow it down the hill to the scrap yard next to the Edgar Thomson. If you wish, you may stay and watch as magnets sort out iron and steel for the mill furnaces."

The kids cheered. "Hurray!" "Swell!" "The scrap drive was a great idea, Charlotte." Her face broke into a smile so wide it hurt. Yes, she really was helping with the war. They all were. Victory!

Charlotte grinned all the way home.

Robbie stood waiting at the back door. "What's wrong with your face? You break it?"

"I'm feeling good, buster. There's a big truck coming Monday to take our scrap down to the mill, and we get to go along. Besides, Ma has a weekend coming and Pa's due home early for once." Charlotte reached into the mailbox and pulled out a letter—a flimsy envelope with a special postmark.

"Look! From Jim!"

"Open it, open it right away," Robbie begged.

She fingered the envelope, tempted. Then she shook her head. "No. Ma and Pa need to be here. It's addressed to them."

"Come on, Charlie." He reached for the letter. "We'll glue it back. They'll never know."

"No. This paper is awful thin. It could tear. Hands off, buster."

She carried the letter inside and propped it up on the kitchen table, where Ma would see it first thing. Instead of a nice note like she'd left on Monday, this morning Ma had simply made a list—*schoolwork, dust, sweep, mop kitchen and bathroom.*

Robbie eyed Ma's note and tried to duck down the hall.

Charlotte grabbed the back of his shirt. "We've got work to do," she told him. "I'm not doing it all."

"But it's the weekend."

She pointed to the letter on the kitchen table. "You think Jim gets weekends off? *Sorry, Captain, can't swab the decks. It's the weekend.*"

Robbie frowned and slumped. "No. But . . ."

Charlotte grinned at him. "Come on, sailor. Time to make this place shipshape."

Between them, they pulled the house into order before Ma came home. She arrived dirty again, and she looked tired, with gray patches under her eyes, but when she saw Jim's letter a smile lit up her face. She scrubbed her hands fast, then peeled the letter open carefully. As Ma began to read, Charlotte noticed holes where the Navy censors had cut out words.

Dear Folks,

 Hope this finds you all well. We sure are busy.
Keeping a ███████ *ship in fighting trim is a lot more*
work than on Pa's tug. And the water—I can't say where
I'm serving, but the water stretches for miles on all sides.
The sky goes on forever.

 When we first came aboard, a few fellas turned
green and hung over the rails for a while, but those high-
water days on the Mon tamed my stomach so I didn't
embarrass myself. My legs handle the ship's roll just fine.

 My shipmates are swell. We've had our moments,
but we're mostly okay. A lot of the guys on my watch
are jokers, so there's always somebody to cheer a fella
up if he's feeling blue or missing his girl. We got one
real young kid who lied about his age to join up, so
we're watching over him pretty close. Funny, we come
from all over, and we haven't known each other long,
but somehow we're more than just pals. Almost like
brothers, I guess.

 Sea rations are nothing to brag about, but every
so often we get a load of ████████████████ ,
a pleasant change. Sure do miss Ma's cooking, though.

 Buster, keep your nose clean. Practice your salutes
and follow orders. If you ever join the Navy you'll find
out just how many orders a fella can get in one day.

 Lottie, hope you're helping Ma and Pa like you
promised. Don't grow up too fast while I'm gone. Wait

*till I get home to invite fellas over, so I can inspect all
your admirers and toss out the stinkers.*

*Ma, Pa, keep the home fires burning. I can't tell you
how often I close my eyes and see all of you sitting around
the kitchen table. That's what we're fighting for—home,
peace, freedom.*

Love to all, your son and brother,
Seaman First Class,
James Henry Campbell, USN

"Thank God." Ma wiped her eyes.

"Darn confetti letter," Robbie said. "How come they
cut out holes this time?"

"He couldn't tell us what kind of ship he's on,"
Charlotte said. "You know that."

"Sure, but they cut out words when he was talking
about food. How come that's a big secret?"

"I don't know," Charlotte said. "Ma?"

Ma looked over the letter again. She blotted her eyes.
"I'm not sure. If I had to guess, I'd say whenever they come
near land, they bring on fresh provisions. If it's pineapples,
he's in the Pacific. Salmon or herring would mean the
North Sea; oranges and lemons, the United States shipping lanes near Florida. So it's classified information."

"I hate those secrets," Robbie grumbled.

"I know," Ma said. "But it's for safety. And we all want
him safe." She turned to Charlotte. "House looks nice,

honey. I'll go run my bath and soak off some of this soot. Then when your Pa gets home, we'll walk uptown and get ourselves some supper. You've cooked plenty this week."

"Burned plenty, too," Robbie said after Ma left. "I think Jim's in the Pacific. It's where I'd want to be. Those tropical islands."

Charlotte bit her lip. "I don't like to think of him so far away. The Atlantic's a lot closer."

"And a lot colder," Robbie argued. "I vote for the Pacific."

"We don't get to vote." Charlotte shook her head. She wasn't about to remind Robbie of all the terrible battles fought on those Pacific islands. But she knew them by heart—Manila, Corregidor, Bataan. The names rumbled through her mind like heavy slag trucks.

They stayed with her, through supper and hot fudge sundaes and beyond, into the night. And in spite of Charlotte's good-luck touch on Jim's blue star, the dream came again. Like before, Jim stood near the ship's rail. Then in an instant he was washed overboard. This time waves grabbed Charlotte too, forcing her to follow Jim.

She thrashed against the icy sea, kicking and pushing, but the swells knocked against her again and again, dragging her under. She struggled to breathe, but instead of air, she drew in water that stung her choking lungs. She coughed and tried to breathe but she was too heavy. She couldn't rise high enough, couldn't get out from under the swells rising up and up on all sides. And then she awoke and could breathe again, but her chest ached, and in her mouth the oily taste of river water lingered.

Odd—river water, not salt. She sat up, startled, and pounded on her chest to clear it. Nothing came out except a raspy cough. She touched her hair, but it was dry. Still, the burning in her lungs felt so real, and the peculiar taste of river water so sour in her mouth.

She sat still in the darkness, trying to calm herself. What was going on? Had the dream of Jim somehow gotten mixed up in her mind with her own accident on the river? Why wouldn't that old memory go away? Sometimes she forgot about it for long stretches of time, but sometimes, like tonight, when the memory of river water tasted strong in her mouth again, it felt like it had all just happened yesterday.

CHAPTER 4
PERSONS UNKNOWN

Charlotte crammed a week's worth of chores into the weekend. She helped Ma with cleaning and laundry and finished most of her schoolwork.

Still, she and Robbie and Betsy managed to collect another load of scrap to haul to school on Monday. The truck was coming, after all, and Charlotte was determined to send it to the mill full of metal.

On Monday morning, Charlotte and Betsy took turns shoving Pa's wheelbarrow filled with metal uphill toward school. Robbie hurried along behind, pulling a heavy load of bent pots and pans in his wagon. Along the sidewalks, other kids carried, dragged, and hauled junk they'd found. Boy, would they fill up that truck.

"Wait till the kids see this. I bet we got the most metal of anybody," Betsy said. "This wheelbarrow's so heavy, my arms are about to fall off."

"Thanks to Mrs. Dubner," Charlotte said. "If her house hadn't been so full . . ."

"Well, it's empty now," Betsy said. "It almost looks nice."

"And don't forget the tulips she gave us," Charlotte said. "Until we cleaned up her yard, those tulips were buried." She shoved the wheelbarrow along the sidewalk and steered it toward the school.

By the time they reached the cellar door, the last bell was ringing and kids were hurrying inside. Was everybody late today? The cellar door was shut, and kids had left baskets and piles of scrap all around instead of hauling it inside. And where was Mr. Willis? She tried the door, but the knob didn't turn. Maybe he was late. Of course, if he hadn't opened the cellar, the kids couldn't put their scrap inside.

"Let's just leave our stuff out here with the rest," Charlotte said. "Maybe we can put it away at recess."

Betsy tugged on her arm. "Come on, wasn't that the last bell? Mrs. Alexander gets mad if we're late."

"Right, Bets. See you after school, Robbie."

When Charlotte and Betsy got to the classroom, Mrs. Alexander looked mad, all right. She stood stiffly beside her desk, frowning. Instead of the usual bustle, kids spoke in whispers. *This couldn't be my fault, could it?* Charlotte wondered. *The whole class wouldn't be acting strange just because Betsy and I were late.* What was going on?

"Do you think it's bad war news?" she asked Betsy. "I didn't hear anything on the radio."

"I haven't heard anything either." Betsy shrugged and looked puzzled.

An uneasy feeling stirred in Charlotte's stomach. If it was more serious than lateness, and it wasn't the war, what was it?

Mrs. Alexander looked around the room, and it felt like she was peering right into Charlotte's mind. Did the teacher know she hadn't finished her arithmetic and was planning to work on it during reading? "Boys and girls, be seated please. I have some very unpleasant news to report."

Kids slid into their seats without noise. It sounded like Mrs. Alexander's news was worse than unfinished fractions.

"Sometime between Friday afternoon and this morning," Mrs. Alexander said, "a person or persons unknown entered the school cellar."

No, Charlotte thought. Please no.

"He, she, or they removed all the metal that this class has collected. From what we can gather, it might be worth a pretty penny if someone tried to sell it," Mrs. Alexander went on. "The principal informed the mill, and today's delivery has been canceled."

"Wow!" "That stinks!" "Doggone!" "No fair!" Voices bubbled up around her, but Charlotte couldn't say a word. Who could have done such a thing?

She looked around. She liked most everybody in her class. Oh sure, Sophie Jaworski could be a pill, but she wouldn't have done this. She'd have gotten too dirty.

Charlotte had watched what Sophie brought in for the drive. One or two tin cans each day, scrubbed as clean as Ma's dishes. And everybody else had worked hard. The Cussick twins had brought in nearly as much scrap as she and Betsy had. Some boys who lived near Braddock Avenue had even collected from the stores. It couldn't be somebody in the class.

Then her eyes fixed on Paul Rossi. His dark hair was overgrown as usual, and he brushed it back from his eyes in a way that looked sneaky to Charlotte. That boy was always getting in trouble. Look at those stories he brought in from the newspapers. He loved crimes and criminals. And stealing was a crime.

"Class, class, please. Settle down." Mrs. Alexander blinked the lights and the room grew quiet. "I'm glad to see that you're all as distressed as I am. This is a deplorable incident, and we will discover the culprit. In the meantime, we need to make a decision—shall we discontinue our scrap drive until the thief is found, or shall we redouble our efforts and make sure to improve our security?"

"Keep going, keep going." The class burst into noise again.

Mrs. Alexander raised her hands. "We'll take a vote. All in favor of continuing to collect metal, please raise your hands."

Every hand shot in the air. Charlotte had never been prouder of her friends.

At recess, even though it was a sunny day and made for games, most kids stood around in clumps. Charlotte and Betsy stood close to the low red-brick wall that enclosed the school yard, whispering. "I feel so bad," Betsy said. "We'll never find as much junk as we did at Mrs. Dubner's."

Before Charlotte could answer, a commotion across the school yard caught her attention. She folded her arms across her chest and frowned. "Look at him, look at that Paul Rossi."

He stood on the seesaw, right in the middle, with his arms flung out. He shifted from side to side, banging the wooden ends down.

"Showing off as usual," Betsy said. "Don't bother with him."

"But don't you see, Bets? Everybody else is talking about the theft. Paul's acting like nothing happened. That's suspicious."

"No, that's Paul. He's a goofball. Hey, Charlotte, do you have to fix dinner for your ma today, or can we start cleaning out my attic for scrap?" Betsy pointed across the yard to the cellar door. "I'd like to refill that room with metal as quick as we can."

"Sure, we can work this afternoon. Ma already fixed a casserole. But Bets, I don't just want to collect more metal. I want to find the scrap we already collected and get it back."

"You think we could find it?"

"I don't know. I'm just so mad! I *hate* what's happened. Stealing's bad enough. But stealing from the war is like *treason*." Her fingers curled into a fist and she smacked it against the rough red bricks. "I'd like to find the person who did this. I'd show him."

Charlotte glared at Paul Rossi, who now hung from the monkey bars. She hadn't noticed before, but he had a bruise on one cheek. From sneaking around in the dark? "There's got to be a way . . ."

"A way to *what*? Charlotte, what are you up to?"

"I'm going to figure out how to catch our thief, that's what. We'll bait a trap, then we'll stand guard and catch him red-handed."

"You're nuts, Charlotte Campbell. You've been reading too many of your ma's mysteries."

But by the time school let out, Charlotte had a plan. She and Betsy talked about it all the way home, figuring out the details.

As they were saying good-bye, Robbie caught up with them. "I know how we can catch the thief!" he said.

Betsy and Charlotte laughed and rolled their eyes at each other. Betsy headed home.

"Stop making faces, Charlie. I do know how to catch him. I have a plan. And it's perfect."

"Let me unlock the door first, buster."

"But, Charlie, it's a great idea. It's sure to work."

Inside, he raced for the bathroom, but he was bouncing with excitement when he got back. "You know down at the mill, how they have those giant magnets?"

"So?" Charlotte set her books on the kitchen table.

"Okay. We need to get one of those magnets. And we'll carry it around and when we feel a tug, we've found the thief's hideout."

"That's ridiculous. Do you know how heavy those magnets are? Your whole class couldn't lift one. It takes a crane."

"We could too lift one. I'm gonna ask Ma. She'll get one for us from the mill. Just you wait and see, Charlotte Campbell. You're not the only person around here with a brain."

The next morning before school, kids again stood around talking quietly about the theft. Charlotte and Betsy stood close together in a sunny corner next to the low brick wall whispering, polishing their plan. "It's good we hadn't started cleaning out our own houses yet. We'll have lots of stuff for bait."

Charlotte pointed to Paul Rossi. He and some other boys were smacking each other's hands. It looked like a game of some sort. "Him. I know he's the one. So all we have to do is make sure he hears us talking about all the junk we've still got in our cellars. How we'll put it outside ready to haul tomorrow night. Then we stay up late and watch. When he shows up to steal it, we catch him."

"Catch who?" Sophie Jaworski asked. "That teacher?"

Charlotte's head snapped up. How had Sophie sneaked up on them? "What teacher?"

Sophie lowered her voice. "Mr. Costa. You know the one. He's new this year. Teaches science to the eighth grade."

"How do you know him, Sophie?" Betsy asked.

"I don't. But my sister has him. He's mean. He really stinks. She and her friends think he's the one. I listened outside her door last night. One of Helen's friends says Mr. Costa could be working for that Italian dictator guy, you know, Mussolini. Mr. Costa is Italian."

"So's Paul Rossi," Charlotte whispered to Betsy. "Could be they're working together."

Betsy shook her head. "A teacher? Come on, Sophie."

"I'm telling you, Helen and her friends have it all figured out. You know how that history teacher, Mr. Debevec, has signed up for the Marines, and Mrs. Alexander's son is training to be a Navy pilot?"

"What's that got to do with Mr. Costa?" Charlotte asked.

"Well, he's young like them, and he's not married either. So how come he didn't sign up to fight?" Sophie lowered her voice to a sly whisper. "Maybe he's a traitor.

Or maybe he's just a yellow-bellied slacker. Either way, he's rotten enough to steal our metal."

"Gosh, Sophie," Betsy said. She shook her head. "Do you really think a teacher would steal the metal?"

"Somebody did. That scrap didn't walk away by itself. So my sister and her friends are gonna keep their eyes on Mr. Costa. Shh." Sophie put her hand to her lips and pretended to turn a key, then walked toward another group of girls.

"That Sophie, she's nuts," Charlotte said. "She's blabbing to the whole school, but she wants us to keep quiet. Besides, it's got to be Paul Rossi."

"I don't know, Charlotte," Betsy began. She stopped talking as two big eighth-grade boys came right up to her.

"You Betsy Schmidt?" one asked.

His voice had an ugly sound. Charlotte reached for her friend's hand and Betsy took it.

"Yes. I'm Betsy."

"We're watching you. Me and my friends, we're gonna keep you in our sights all the time. You and your Kraut family."

"Wait a minute," Charlotte said. "What do you mean, *Kraut*?"

The boy sneered at her. "Lousy German. Stinkin' Nazi. You understand them words?"

"But Betsy's not—" Charlotte began. Betsy squeezed her hand tightly.

The other boy stuck his finger right under Betsy's nose. "You tell us. If you ain't a Kraut, where'd you get your last name?"

"My great-great-grandparents came from Germany. But that was a long time ago."

"See." The first boy glared at Charlotte. Then he turned his attention to Betsy. "It's just plain rotten, how they let scum like you into the U. S. of A. Don't make another move, or you'll be sorry."

"Who are you calling scum?" Charlotte demanded. "You leave Betsy alone. Her brother's fighting for the U. S. of A."

She tugged Betsy's hand and they ducked away from the boys toward the door.

Betsy's face had turned pale and her blue eyes looked wet.

"Come on, don't listen to them," Charlotte said. "They don't know anything. The one in the blue sweater, Frankie Zalenchak, he's a bully, always picking on younger kids. And that Danny Merkow just sticks with Frankie because he likes to sound tough."

"But they called me a Kraut, Charlotte. I can't help my last name." The tears spilled over and Betsy rubbed at them with her fists.

Charlotte flung her arm around Betsy's shaking shoulders. "They're crazy, Bets. Your family's been in America for a long time. If anybody's a foreigner here, they are."

She turned and glared at the boys, but they had their backs to her and couldn't see.

"Oh, no. Look, Charlotte. They're going after my cousin Pete. They got into an argument with Pete last week, and now it's starting up again. He's got a temper. They're going to get him in trouble. Charlotte, we've got to—"

The bell rang, and just in time. Another minute and war would have erupted in the school yard.

As they marched back to their classroom, they passed the cellar door. Mr. Willis knelt on the floor with a screwdriver in his hand. As she stepped closer, Charlotte could see that he was installing a new lock on the door. Well, good.

"Look, Bets," she whispered. "The new metal we collect will stay safe. We'll collect so much, nobody will dare say another word about your last name."

Betsy shook her head like she didn't believe Charlotte. "What if they talk to their parents? What if somebody says something to my dad at the mill? He's got a temper just like Pete's."

"All the more reason for us to collect the most metal of anybody. And find the real thief. Once we catch him, we'll be heroes. Come on, we'll drop the first hints now, when we get close to Paul Rossi's desk."

"I don't know," Betsy said.

"Well, I do." Charlotte stepped quickly past Sophie and the Cussick twins. She was practically leaning on

Paul's desk. "Okay, Betsy, let's stack it all in my back alley tomorrow night. Wednesday," she added loudly, just in case Paul wasn't listening the first time. "We'll have a ton of metal by then. We'll show them. Nobody can beat the team of Campbell and Schmidt."

CHAPTER 5

SUSPICIOUS CHARACTERS

The commotion didn't stop when Charlotte got home. Robbie and his friends had been busy, too. "I got two ideas about the thief," he announced to Charlotte. "Two real good ones."

"Oh, come on," Charlotte said. "You're in fourth grade." She unlocked the back door. How did nine-year-olds come up with suspects?

"Just 'cause we're smaller than you doesn't mean we're dumb." He stomped inside behind her and slammed down his books on the kitchen table.

"Okay, who's on your list?"

"I'm not gonna tell."

Oh, great. Mr. Stubborn. "Please, Robbie. You were good at finding scrap. You might be good at finding the thief, too."

"You mean it?"

"Come on, tell me. Who knows, if you're right, we might catch the thief in the act. How about that?"

He grinned. "Okay. Most of my class thinks one thing. But I'm not ready to make up my mind yet. I'm still looking at the clues."

"What clues? Who does your class think took the metal?"

"Wagon Willie."

"What?"

"You heard me. Wagon Willie. You know, the janitor."

"You mean Mr. Willis? Why would he . . ."

"He already goes around collecting stuff. All summer long, he pushes that big wagon of his around the streets collecting stuff to sell."

"And you think he took our metal?"

"I'm not sure yet. But he could have. He's always around school. Some kids say he sleeps there. And he's, you know, strange."

Charlotte shook her head. "He just has trouble getting his words out sometimes. I don't think he'd steal. He's always nice to us." She frowned. She'd known Mr. Willis ever since she'd started school. A lot of kids made fun of him, but Charlotte thought he was nice.

Once in second grade she'd gotten sick in the hall and he'd cleaned it up. She'd said she was sorry, but Mr. Willis had shaken his head and smiled. "N-n-no, Missy. Can't help getting sick. F-f-feel better."

And she had. No, Mr. Willis couldn't be the thief. She refused to believe it. "You said you had two good ideas, Robbie. Who else?"

"There's this kid in my class, Tommy Stankowski. I don't like him anyway. He's always dirty and he talks rough."

"You think a fourth grader took all that stuff? Impossible. It's too heavy."

"Okay, maybe it's a long shot, but he could have had help. Listen, Charlie, he brought a lunch pail to school that looked exactly like the one we found in old Mrs. Dubner's cellar. It was even busted in the same place."

"That's ridiculous. Half the kids in school have metal lunch pails. And I bet a lot of them are broken. Nope, *I'm* betting on Paul Rossi, buster. And we're going to set a trap to catch him. Want to help?"

"A trap? Sure."

As soon as Charlotte had changed clothes, she headed to Betsy's house and knocked on the door. Mrs. Schmidt answered. "She's not feeling too good, Charlotte. And to tell you the truth, neither am I. She'll see you tomorrow." Betsy's ma looked tired and didn't even try to smile.

Charlotte couldn't blame her. The way those eighth graders had gone after Betsy, it was wicked. She told Robbie about it when she returned home and they started down the steps to their own cellar.

"For real? Some guys said Betsy was the thief? And called her a Kraut? That's dumb."

"You want more dumbness? Sophie Jaworski thinks one of the teachers did it."

"Which one? How come?"

"Mr. Costa, because he's got an Italian name." A shadow of guilt flitted across Charlotte's mind. She'd said the same thing about Paul Rossi. That maybe he and Mr. Costa were in it together because they were Italian. Her cheeks felt hot as she remembered.

Well, that wasn't the real reason she suspected him, she told herself. With all those crime stories, he made himself look guilty. "Come on, Robbie. Let's start in the back room. The more metal we collect, the better trap we can build."

Instead of hauling the day's collection to school the next morning, Charlotte and Robbie stacked it in the alley behind their house. Bait.

She pointed it out to Betsy on the way to school.

"That's nice, Charlotte," she said. Her voice was quiet.

"You're still upset, aren't you?"

"Wouldn't you be?"

"Yeah. But you can't let those dumb boys get to you. They don't have one brain between the two of them. Come on, let's get to school fast. So we can talk real loud about our stash of metal in front of you-know-who. If we catch him, that'll take care of Zalenchak and Merkow."

"Yeah, maybe." Betsy still didn't sound convinced.

That made Charlotte even more determined. She walked faster. When they got to the school yard, the early bell hadn't even rung and kids were milling around. Charlotte spotted Paul Rossi and headed toward him, dragging Betsy along.

"Hi, Paul," she said. "Find any pots and pans lately?"

"Some. How about you?"

"Lots. We found so much, we can't carry it," Charlotte said. "We'll have to wait till Betsy's pa can drive it to school."

"Oh yeah?"

"Yeah. And we'll have even more by tomorrow. If you don't believe me, just take a look in the alley behind our house."

"Maybe I will and maybe I won't. You know, you've got to watch out for dark alleys. Two guys busted out of jail yesterday down in Pittsburgh. They could be headed this way. Don't say I didn't warn you." He raised his eyebrows, then walked away.

Charlotte frowned. The early bell rang and Betsy tugged on her sweater, pulling her toward some girls in their class who were stretching out a jump rope. "Come on, you two," they called. "You want to try double Dutch?"

"Sure," Betsy said.

Sophie Jaworski turned and stopped them as they got close to the girls with the rope. "Charlotte, Betsy, what's going on? I saw you talking to that Paul Rossi. If I didn't know better, I'd think one of you had a crush on him."

Betsy shook her head. "Not me."

"Me either," Charlotte said. She stuck out her tongue and wrinkled her nose. "He's the worst boy in our class."

"That's what I've always thought," Sophie said. "Still, you went over to him. You better watch out, Charlotte. People will talk . . ."

"Forget it, Sophie. I've got better things to do." Charlotte and Betsy joined the group of girls and took turns jumping.

When the bell rang again, Charlotte and Betsy shoved through the crowd and up the worn stone steps into the main hallway, where little kids' drawings of spring flowers decorated the walls. Sophie's words still bounced around in Charlotte's mind. A crush on Paul Rossi? She couldn't get far enough away from Sophie and her crazy ideas. As they reached the door to their classroom, Frankie Zalenchak and Danny Merkow practically knocked them down.

"Watch where you're going, you big bullies," Charlotte called after them.

Betsy turned to Charlotte, a worried look in her eyes. "What are they doing here? The eighth graders use the stairs at the other end of the hall. I don't like this one bit."

"You can't let them get on your nerves, Bets. If they see you're scared, they'll bother you more. Come on, Mrs. Alexander is waiting for us."

When she walked into her classroom, Charlotte sniffed. Something smelled funny. The smell grew stronger as she and Betsy moved down the row toward their desks. "Hey, what is that smell, anyway?" she asked.

She was about to slip into her seat when she caught sight of Betsy, pale like somebody had painted her face with flour.

"No! Oh, Charlotte, no!" Betsy dropped her books and covered her eyes.

Charlotte stepped closer and looked into Betsy's opened desk. The smell hit her nose like a stink bomb. Somebody—two somebodies, Charlotte figured—had dumped a big can of sauerkraut all over the inside of Betsy's desk.

The sixth grade got to play dodgeball for an hour that morning while Mr. Willis cleaned up the mess and brought in a new desk for Betsy. Frankie Zalenchak and Danny Merkow got kicked out of school for the rest of the week.

Mrs. Alexander asked Betsy if she'd like to go home, but Betsy refused. "I didn't do anything wrong," she said. "I'll stay."

"Good for you," Charlotte said. "You're not letting those bullies turn you into mush."

And Betsy didn't. For a soft-looking girl, with rosy cheeks and pale brown hair, Betsy flung the ball that morning like she was training for the dodgeball Olympics. Charlotte felt sorry for the kids in the middle.

By lunchtime, the whole school was buzzing about the sauerkraut incident. The sixth and seventh grades stuck up for the Schmidt family, angry that Betsy and her cousin Pete were being treated like enemies. The eighth grade was split. The boys stuck with Zalenchak and Merkow, but the girls thought they were bullies. Besides, according to Sophie, the eighth-grade girls still believed that Mr. Costa was the thief.

"They're going to get some evidence on him. This week," Sophie promised. "They have plans, but I couldn't hear what. I'll keep spying on my sister and her friends to see what they're up to."

Charlotte shook her head. Anybody who thought she had a crush on Paul Rossi couldn't be trusted. She'd keep to her original plan and make sure Paul heard again about the big pile of metal she'd collected. She'd catch him tonight, red-handed, and prove Betsy innocent in the bargain.

Late that night, she sat in the dark and peered out her bedroom window. In the distance, factory lights lit up the riverbanks as the Mon flowed on, a wide black ribbon, smooth and treacherous, broken only by the tiny star-points of buoy lights.

She shifted her attention back to the dark alley below. Among the shadows, she could just make out the heap of scrap she and Robbie had carefully piled up, ready to come crashing down at the slightest touch. Next door, Betsy was awake and watching, too. They were probably the only people awake in the whole neighborhood, Charlotte thought. But they were ready. They each had a flashlight for signaling. Charlotte had borrowed Jim's baseball bat and propped it right next to the window.

At about eleven, Charlotte heard a loud, clattering clank. The thief! She pressed her nose to the glass, but all she could see were black trees, spidery bushes, and the shadowy pile of bait. She flashed her light out the side window twice, toward Betsy's house, and waited. No reply.

Had Betsy fallen asleep? Charlotte signaled again. Nothing. Maybe she should get Robbie. But he slept like a stone. And she didn't dare wake Ma or Pa . . .

Charlotte's mouth went dry. This couldn't be happening. She and Betsy had made plans to catch the thief together. Now she was all by herself. She peered out the window.

What if Paul wasn't working alone? What if it wasn't even Paul out there? Suddenly his warning popped back into her head. Watch out for dark alleys, he'd said. Hadn't two men just broken out of jail in Pittsburgh? Would they come to Braddock?

No, of course they wouldn't. Besides, if her trap was working, she couldn't give up the chance to catch the thief red-handed. Heart pounding, she tucked the flashlight under her arm, grabbed the baseball bat, and eased open the door to her room. On tiptoe she made it to the top of the stairs, then crept down through the inky blackness and into the kitchen. With shaking fingers, she eased open the back door. The night air chilled her face; as she tiptoed out to the porch her bare feet felt damp. One step at a time, she inched toward the alley.

Something hissed. Then something yowled and brushed her leg. She jumped backward. With a crash, two silvery cats sprang from the scrap pile and bounded over the fence into Mrs. Dubner's backyard.

A light went on there, and Charlotte heard a voice. "Hush, you silly rascals. Hush now. There, that's better."

Cats! Crazy old Mrs. Dubner's cats. There should be laws to keep people like her from acting so strange and scaring the neighbors, Charlotte thought.

She took deep breaths and tried to make her heart stop racing. Cats, just cats. She flashed her light on the alley, to make sure. All she could see were an old cast-iron sink, a rusty bucket, and a mess of tin cans. She re-piled the metal and crept carefully back to her room to watch. Paul Rossi might still show up tonight, she told herself.

It took half an hour for Charlotte's heart to return to its regular speed. In another half hour, she was yawning.

Sometime after midnight, she gave up and crawled into bed.

At first light, she tumbled out of the covers and checked the window. Her scrap pile sat in the alley, undisturbed. Darn it, anyway. Why hadn't that rotten Paul Rossi snapped up her bait? She fell back into bed and tried to make a new plan as she waited for the rest of the family to wake up.

No brilliant ideas came that morning, not in bed, not at breakfast, not on the way to school with Betsy. When she reached the school yard, more bad news waited.

"Somebody came back to the cellar last night," Marnie Cussick announced. "Teachers are in there now, looking around."

"Somebody stole our scrap again," her sister said. "It's wicked and rotten."

No! Charlotte felt like somebody had set her on fire. She shoved her way through the crowd of kids gathered near the cellar door, to where Paul Rossi stood alone, watching the angry faces. "Now I know why you didn't grab the scrap from my alley. You had other plans last night, didn't you?"

"What are you talking about, Charlotte? You calling me a thief?" He stared at her hard, without blinking.

"What if I am?" She stepped closer to him. "You skip school sometimes. Don't deny it. And you're always getting sent to the principal and bringing in those crime stories."

"So what? That doesn't mean I'd mess with the war. I'm no traitor. I got two brothers in the Marines."

Betsy came up behind her and took Charlotte's hand. "You have brothers in the war, too? I didn't know that."

Charlotte stepped back. She hadn't known it either. She swallowed. "But still . . . where did you get that bruise on your cheek?"

"Mind your own business." He swiped his cheek and glared as the bell rang, ending the argument but not Charlotte's suspicions.

Still, to be fair, right after the Pledge of Allegiance she made a complete list of people who might have stolen the metal—Paul Rossi, Mr. Costa, Mr. Willis, even that little kid in Robbie's class. She refused to put Betsy's name on the list. But at the bottom she wrote down Zalenchak and Merkow. Were they smart enough to accuse Betsy so nobody would suspect them? Sure. So maybe they should take Paul's spot at the top of her list. Maybe, and maybe not. Either way, she'd have to set another trap. A better one.

She slipped the list into her history book so Mrs. Alexander wouldn't think it was a note and read it out loud. A good detective couldn't let her suspects know what she was up to, could she?

CHAPTER 6
STITCHES

After lunch, the little kids were going inside as Charlotte's class was heading out. Robbie popped out of line and stuck a note in her hand.

Charlotte. Rick Maloney found an old dump. Buried treasure, lots of cans, up at the end of Second Avenue. Let's go after school. Robbie

Charlotte had on her oldest skirt, one that was too tight, anyway, so Ma wouldn't mind if she worked awhile without changing. They'd lose half an hour if they went home first. "Okay. Meet you there," she called as Robbie's class marched inside.

After school, she and Betsy walked along Second Avenue. The neighborhood was west of theirs by a few blocks, but it looked about the same. All the houses in the flats along the river were lined up in rows, with small yards and alleys along the back. If you wanted fancy in Braddock, you had to climb the hill.

At the end of Second Avenue, Charlotte could see a weedy, junk-filled vacant lot with several small boys hard at work. On the sidewalk they'd lined up buckets and wagons and filled them with old rusty cans. Robbie and his friend Rick stood in the middle of the vacant lot wrestling with what looked like a door from an old car.

"That's real heavy. Let us help," she offered.

She stepped carefully around an old icebox and some broken bottles. Robbie was grabbing the top of the old car door. Rick tugged at the handle.

"We need to move this old tire out of the way first," Betsy said. "It's jamming the door."

Charlotte bent to grab the tire. Nasty, greenish water dumped out when she and Betsy lifted it. "Come on, let's roll this to the sidewalk for the eighth graders' tire drive. Even if we're mad at them, the tires will help the war."

When they got to the sidewalk, Charlotte let the tire flop down. As she straightened her back, she found herself looking at Paul Rossi. "What are you doing here?" she asked in surprise.

"What, is there a law against standing on the sidewalk? I live nearby. What about you?"

She shrugged. "Just collecting scrap. My brother and his friends—"

"Hey, that's a big door they're lifting. Want some help?"

No, Charlotte wanted to say. You'll only steal this too. But if he really did have brothers in the Marines, would he? Besides, Robbie and Rick were getting nowhere with that door.

"Okay. The door is pretty heavy."

Paul, Charlotte, and Betsy stepped back around the icebox. With five kids lifting, they freed the car door and lugged it to the sidewalk.

"Let her down easy," Paul said. "One, two—"

Something must have slipped. Charlotte held tight to the door bottom, but the top clanked to the ground.

Robbie reached and tried to stop it, then yelled. "Oww!"

"What?" Charlotte dropped the door and grabbed for Robbie's hand. Blood dripped all over the sidewalk. "Gosh, Robbie! Oh, geez. Somebody help us."

Before she could even think what to do, Paul Rossi had ripped off his shirt and was wrapping it tightly around Robbie's hand. "Come on, kid. We'd better get you to the hospital."

"Wait! Our doctor's office is right up on the avenue. It's closer," said Charlotte, staring at the shirt. Blood was soaking through. Robbie's blood. The muscles in Charlotte's legs went soft and she swayed. Betsy grabbed hold of her and put an arm around her waist.

"Lead the way." Paul picked up Robbie. "We'll make better time if I carry you," he said. "And you can holler if you want. I sure would."

"Five stitches." Robbie waved a white gauze hand under Charlotte's nose.

She ducked back. It looked like a mummy's hand from a creepy movie.

"It's neat," he bragged. "I'd show you, but they wrapped my hand up so you can't see."

"I . . . I'll see it later. Can we go home now?"

"Did they give you a tetanus shot?" Paul asked. "Last time I got sewed up, they poked me with a needle big enough for a horse."

"Right here." Robbie pointed to his left arm. "I told them to save the shot for a soldier, but they said they had plenty."

Beside her, Betsy shivered. "I hate shots."

"Me too." Charlotte studied Robbie's face. He was grinning, but his skin looked pale. "Can you make it home?"

"I'm no baby."

"I'll come too," Paul offered.

Charlotte shook her head. "Thanks, but . . ."

"No trouble. Those shots can make you pretty woozy."

A nurse gave Charlotte a sheet of instructions for Ma and explained how to clean and wrap Robbie's hand. He'd need to come back in a few days so they could take out his stitches.

They walked home slowly. At every corner, Paul made Robbie stop and sit down on somebody's steps and rest before starting the next block. Charlotte wanted to hurry home so she could wash the blood off her hands and clothes, but Paul seemed to know what he was doing.

When they finally got home, Robbie flopped onto the sofa. Charlotte headed into the kitchen to wash up, and Betsy followed her.

"Robbie's pretty pale," Betsy began. "You don't look so good either, Charlotte. You want me to get my mother?"

Charlotte checked the kitchen clock as she scrubbed the blood off her hands. Ma would be home soon, and they'd have some explaining to do. She shook her head. "Thanks, Bets, but we'll be okay."

Betsy left by the kitchen door. Charlotte dried her hands and slipped into the living room in time to see Paul stick a pillow under Robbie's arm. "Keep it high," he said. "Won't hurt so much."

"How do you know all this stuff?" Charlotte asked.

Paul seemed startled to see her. "Me and my brothers, we've been stitched some. No big deal."

Suddenly it was a big deal to Charlotte. She'd accused Paul Rossi of stealing, and then he'd turned around and taken care of Robbie. He'd behaved real nice, too, not tough like he acted at school.

"I'm sorry," she began. Her cheeks burned, but she refused to let that stop her. "What I said in school. I was wrong. You're not a bad guy, a thief."

Paul shrugged. "Don't make a fuss, Charlotte. At school now, with everybody accusing people . . . Well, when I think about my brothers off fighting, it makes all this seem cheap."

"You're not mad at me?"

"I was. But geez. Your folks will light into both of you tonight. That's enough for one day." He slapped Robbie on the shoulder and stuck out his hand to Charlotte. "Pals? I'll help you haul stuff to school if you want, since he's on the wounded list."

Charlotte shook his hand. "Thanks." As he left, she stared after him. Who'd have thought she'd ever be pals with Paul Rossi? Or that he could be nice?

Half an hour later, Ma came home. After she checked Robbie's hand and made sure he was okay, she glared. "No more collecting metal for you, buster. You either, Charlotte."

"But, Ma . . . It's for the war."

"It's too dangerous," Ma said. "I've got enough on my mind, worrying about Jim."

"But, Ma, it's for Jim. Could I please keep working? I'll be really careful. I'll wear gloves."

"I'll think about it. But neither of you picks up as much as a tin can until I decide. Hear me?"

"Yes, Ma."

"Buster?"

Robbie didn't reply. He'd fallen asleep.

With Robbie's hand needing to heal, all the chores landed on Charlotte. Ma probably didn't mean it as a punishment, but it felt like one. Washing clothes on a rainy Friday afternoon, then pinning them up in the cellar to dry—that wasn't Charlotte's idea of a weekend. Neither was cleaning and ironing all day Saturday. But she couldn't complain; Ma worked twice as hard.

When Sunday dawned, it was the third rainy day in a row. Charlotte made her way to the kitchen, where her parents read the paper over coffee.

"I've got a sweet roll still warm in the oven for you," Ma said. She stood and gave Charlotte a hug. She pointed to Robbie, who was reading the funny pages. "Had to hide it from that brother of yours. Something about stitches seems to make fellas hungry."

"Thanks, Ma. I'll help you with the cooking after church. It's a mean day outside."

"Bad weather or not, I've got lines to check," Pa interrupted. "That Rowley boy just joined the Army, so I'm down a deckhand." He turned to Charlotte. "I need you on the *Rose* this afternoon."

Her stomach tightened. "But, Pa, can't Robbie help?"

"He'd get his bandages all wet."

Robbie looked up from the comics. "I want to go. Please, Pa. I'll be careful. I can wrap my hand."

"You can come if you want, but you can't work. You'll just keep us company. Lottie, I really need you today."

Pa folded up his paper and went to dress for church.

That morning in church, Charlotte prayed as she always did—for the war to end, for Jim and all the soldiers and sailors to come home safe. She added a couple extra prayers at the end.

"Please, God, forgive me for letting Robbie get hurt. And for thinking and saying bad stuff about Paul Rossi." She closed her eyes tighter. "And if I have to help on the boat, could it maybe stop raining?"

Either God wasn't listening, or he'd decided that a little rain was good penance, for the clouds only got grayer as afternoon came and she, Pa, and Robbie walked to the docks. Since the war had started, Sunday was about the only day the docks were quiet. Still, there were signs of activity inside the nearby mill buildings. Charlotte shivered and wished she could help indoors instead of on the tug in the rain.

They neared the mooring where the *Rose* bobbed in rough water, shedding rain like an oversized duck. The *Rose* wasn't a big tug like the ones that hauled long strings of barges from the Great Lakes to New Orleans. But she wasn't small, either. The engines took up most of her wide belly, the pilothouse sat above the front, and tall exhaust stacks poked up behind, making her nearly as high as she was long. With her blunt nose hitched close to the dock, she looked clumsy and bulky, but on the water with a barge or two in tow, she was shipshape enough. If a person cared for ships.

Pa climbed aboard and held out his hand, first to
Robbie, then to Charlotte. She looked down as he swung
her onto the deck. High water, rushing and brown with all
the rain. The worst time to be on the river.

"We need to check all the lines and all the cables,"
Pa said. He unlocked the door, which led up to the pilothouse and down to the engine room. "Let's get oilskins on
so we don't get completely soaked." He opened a storage
locker and pulled out three yellow slickers, then went
below to the engine room.

Charlotte shrugged into the oilskin, which felt chill
and clammy. She stared out at the choppy river. Raindrops
pocked the surface, and gusts of wind whipped up waves.
A metallic, oily taste came to her tongue.

Robbie scowled at her. "What's the matter, Charlie?
You scared? Come on, you can swim, even if it took you
forever to learn." He made it sound like he was the older
one and she was a dumb little kid.

"I'm not scared. I just don't like high water." Charlotte
frowned, remembering. After the accident, Jim had dragged
her to the Carnegie Library's big indoor pool after school
for months. "No sister of mine's gonna drown," he'd said.
He'd been real patient with her, though. All along, he'd
told her it wasn't her fault she was a sinker, too skinny to
float. And finally, she'd learned. But swimming in a pool
wasn't the same as facing high water on the river.

She looked at Robbie's sturdy, solid shape. He and Jim

took after Pa, born loving water and swimming like fish. She, on the other hand, had gotten Ma's long, lean bones. Heavy bones.

Pa returned from the engine room below.

"Can I use the spyglass, Pa? While you and Charlie check lines?"

"Don't see why not. Go on, sit up in my chair and keep watch. We'll snap on the radio, too. You holler down if you spot trouble."

Trouble? Charlotte looked around at the surging river. She followed Pa to the front, where several thick ropes lay in neat coils. On the port side, he lifted one, stretched it out, and rewound it, carefully checking for worn spots. It was important work, Charlotte knew, even if she didn't like doing it. A frayed rope could mean a lost barge. She knelt on the starboard side and checked her first coil.

The lines were soaked with rain, and cold. The wet made the twisted hemp swell up even thicker than usual. Her fingers ached by the time she'd re-coiled the first one. Heavy work, but at least she didn't have to look at the river. She glanced up to the window of the pilothouse. Robbie had Pa's spyglass out and was studying the southern riverbank. She moved to a second coil, then a third.

The front lines and cables were all strong, so she and Pa moved to the stern, where Pa found a mooring line unraveling in the middle. She helped him secure a new line, holding the thick hemp rope as he worked the knots.

"Hold tighter, Lottie," he said. "You're letting her slip."

"It's hard, Pa. My hands are cold."

"Put on gloves then. Should be a pair in your pockets. If this knot gives, a whole string of barges could drift off. You know that, girl."

Charlotte pulled on the heavy leather gloves. They were damp and too large, but they did make the rope less slick.

Pa slipped the last loop into place and tested the line. He nodded. "Good and tight. Thanks, Lottie."

Great, they were done. Charlotte could go home now and get warm and dry. This hadn't taken too long, after all. Just then she heard a shout.

Above her head, Robbie leaned out of the pilothouse window, waving his arms. "Pa, Charlie! Trouble on the river. Barges loose upstream! On the radio they're calling all the tugs to help!"

"Not us. We can't . . ." Charlotte began, but she knew better. When trouble came on the river, all hands pitched in. There wasn't much worse trouble than loose barges. If the barges were fully loaded, they could ram and destroy anything in their path. "Oh, Pa," she cried.

But Pa didn't hear. He'd already run for the stairs and the radio, leaving her alone and shivering in the stern.

CHAPTER 7
RUNAWAYS ON THE RIVER

Charlotte made her way up the stairs to the pilothouse. Pa shoved his spyglass into her hands. "Stay topside and keep watch on the river. If you see any runaway barges, come get me. I have to fire up the boiler."

"But, Pa, you don't have a crew. Just Robbie and me."

"You'll do." Pa turned to Robbie. "Come on, buster, think you can watch the steam gauge and shovel in a little coal?"

"Sure, Pa." Robbie grinned. "And Charlie, look, in the bend of the river. Look with the glass." He pointed to the far northern bank of the Mon. "A pile of metal."

Pa clattered down the steps, with Robbie following right behind. Charlotte let herself sink into Pa's captain's chair. She heard thumps below as Pa opened the firebox and started to shovel in coal.

She scanned the river with the glass. No sign of barges,

just bits of trash carried by the rushing water. After a spell of rain like this, the banks always got littered. She turned the glass to where Robbie had pointed. Sure enough, a bigger-than-usual pile of junk covered a steep part of the bank. But who cared? Within minutes the *Rose* would be fired up and rolling with no real crew.

"Down here, Lottie," Pa shouted. "I need you on deck."

She tightened her oilskin and stepped down to join Pa. Rain spattered her face. The deck felt greasy underfoot.

He pointed to one of the coiled mooring lines—a heavy rope with a loop at the end. "Stand here, at the front. The minute we spot a runaway barge, I'll steer up close. You drop this line around the barge's mooring pin, then haul her up tight, and we'll tow her back to the docks, slick as a whistle."

"But, Pa . . ." There was no railing around the flat nose of the tug. Only a few feet of deck and then—river. A single slip and . . .

"Easy as catching a fish, sweetheart," Pa said. He pinched her cheek with wet, cold fingers.

"Pa, coal barges aren't fish, they're whales. I can't—"

"'Course you can. I'll keep my window open so we can shout to each other. Hold tight now, and cast off when I get her humming."

Inside the heavy gloves, Charlotte's hands felt clammy and sore. Rain pounded the deck. Through the soles of her feet she could feel the engines begin to pump.

Pa signaled and she cast off, loosening the heavy ropes that bound the tug to the dock pilings. Then she crept to the middle of the tug's front. There at least she was farthest from the roiling brown water. She watched the banks as Pa brought the *Rose* around and headed her upstream. The engines hummed as the *Rose* bit into the current.

From port to starboard, she checked the river. If only it weren't Sunday, there'd be plenty of other boats to help. But today only the big working boats would be hauling, and they could be miles away. So it was up to her and Pa. *Darn rain. Why did barges always break free?* It happened every spring with high water—a cable would snap and barges would get loose. Why didn't somebody tie them down tighter? Or could it be they tied them too tight?

"Lottie, look ahead, starboard bank," Pa shouted.

She peered through the rain. A dark shape hovered on the horizon, hulking and huge. Pa steered the *Rose* toward starboard. As they chugged closer, Charlotte could see more clearly. It wasn't one barge, it was two, and both of them piled high with coal.

She clenched her fingers and turned toward the pilot-house. "Pa, what do we do?"

He motioned her toward the starboard mooring lines. "Grab your line and get ready to throw it. I'll bring her as close as I can."

"But, Pa, two barges . . ." Roped together side by side,

they were bigger than a football field, at least sixty feet wide and three times that long.

Pa waved her on.

She inched out, looked upriver, and blinked hard. Hundreds of tons of coal were headed straight toward them. Sure, Pa could steer the *Rose,* but those barges were runaways. Charlotte knew that full barges could float any which way. They had no rudders, no controls at all. Her stomach clenched. What if they rammed into the *Rose?* She could nearly taste the water.

"They're loaded, Pa!"

"Better full than empty," he called back. "Empties flop around more."

Pa steered closer. Rain soaked Charlotte's hair and her gloves. She uncoiled the heavy line and held the loop in both hands, watching. Fifty feet, then twenty-five. Her breath came in fast, short bursts that burned her lungs.

She squinted through the heavy rain until she could see the mooring pins on the nearest barge. Darn, they were small. They looked like coffee cans at this distance. How close would Pa dare get? How far could she throw the line? She looked down at the rushing brown river. Mistake. Her stomach heaved.

Pa eased the *Rose* closer. She could see a spill of coal along the near edge of the barge. Water surged in the gap between tug and barge, like the river was angry at being trapped.

"Now!" Pa shouted.

She flung the line out. The loop end snaked out like a lasso, then splashed into the river. She hauled it in again, colder and wetter than before. She'd missed the first pin.

"Lottie, go closer."

She took a deep breath and half a step forward. She tossed the rope toward the second mooring pin as Pa steered parallel to the huge barge. Her line thumped the side, then splashed again. The angry river slapped at the side of the tug and pulled the rope under.

Her feet could feel the *Rose*'s engine slowing as Pa kept her alongside the barge. The third mooring pin was coming. If she missed this one, they'd have to pull away and start over. She took another half step forward. There was nothing to hold onto but a cold, slippery rope. Churning water gushed between the tug and the barge. They were edging so close a person would be squished if she went overboard.

She held her breath, then threw the line as hard and as straight as she could. The loop snagged the pin, flopped, then held.

She yanked the line tight and forced the heavy rope into a hitching loop, and then another and another, until the first barge was secure against the nose of the tug.

"Good work, Lottie," Pa called. She sidestepped away from the edge, feeling the shift of weight as the tug's engine began to haul at the corner of the barge. Charlotte knew what Pa was doing. The two barges were still dangerous, floating alongside the tug and hitched in only one place. Pa had to line up the *Rose* square behind the barges, so he could push them.

He steered the tug around slowly. The engine rumbled in protest. "Get ready to secure another line, Lottie. Port side, so we can balance these babies," Pa shouted.

"I can't," she whispered. But she knew she didn't have a choice. An inch at a time, she made her way across the slippery deck to the port-side mooring line.

When Pa finally got the *Rose* lined up behind the barges, Charlotte dropped the port line over the second barge's closest mooring pin. As she hauled in the line to secure it, the palms of her hands stung.

Pa called her up to the pilothouse to join him. "That was some job, sailor," he said, pulling her into his arms and hugging her tight. "How are your hands?"

"Sore." She stepped back and peeled off her wet gloves. Red lines cut into the palms of her hands. "Oh, Pa, I'm no sailor. I was so scared."

"Scared or not, you came through." He hugged her again. Then he turned to his rudder sticks and began to steer. The *Rose*'s engines thrummed and groaned. Slowly the pair of barges nosed out into the middle of the muddy Mon.

Back at the dock, Pa pulled three short blasts on the whistle to let Ma know they were coming home soon. He tied up the tug and both barges until the barge owners could come the next day to collect their coal. Then he went below to shut down the engines.

Robbie bounded up to the deck with Pa. "Wow! Charlie, Pa says you're a hero! You roped two barges. Me too! I kept the steam coming. Wow, look at those barges." He grabbed Charlotte's hand and tugged her closer to the starboard side.

She held back.

"What's the matter? How come you're shaking?"

She closed her eyes. "I'm just cold," she said. "Freezing. I was on deck in the rain while you were warm and dry in the engine room."

As they walked home, Robbie talked nonstop about the barges and the pile of metal he'd seen and how, once he got his stitches out, he'd start collecting again. "I'm gonna keep helping with the war," he bragged.

"You already have," Pa told him. "You and your sister both." He pointed upriver toward the railroad bridge as a train whistled in the distance. "If we hadn't caught the barges . . ." His voice quit.

Charlotte turned toward him. "What, Pa, what if we hadn't?"

"River's up and running," he said, pointing. "At the speed they were traveling, those loads could have knocked out the bridge. You know how important bridges are, especially that railroad bridge."

Charlotte looked where Pa pointed. As she stared,

a train rounded into sight. The last time she'd looked at that bridge there'd been a train on it too. Jim's train, full of soldiers and sailors.

Sunday Night, May 17, 1942

Dear Jim,

I haven't written for a while. First, nothing much was going on. Then we got real busy and it was hard to find time. Now I'd better write. So much has happened, if I don't write soon, I'll forget parts.

This all started about three weeks ago. The President got on the radio and talked about the home front and everybody pitching in to help win the war. Even us kids. Well, you'll be proud to know I figured out a way—we started a scrap metal drive at school. It was going swell, too.

Then, guess what? Some low-down sneak stole all the metal. We have lots of suspects and we're watching them close. We'll have to work fast, for school will be out soon. Next letter I hope to tell you the wicked thief is in jail.

I think Ma was about ready to throw ME in jail last Thursday. Robbie's been helping us look for junk, and he's good at it. This will be no surprise to you since he's raided your room for marbles and stuff to use in his boats plenty of times.

Anyway, on Thursday we went to a dump at the end of Second Avenue. He and another kid found an old car door. We were all hauling it out of the dump, but we dropped it and Robbie sliced up his hand on some broken glass in the car window. He got five stitches and a tetanus shot. Ma says no more scrapping for us.

Now here's the biggest surprise of all. Remember how every spring a few barges pop loose at high water? It happened again today while Pa had Robbie and me helping on the Rose. Guess who lassoed not one but two coal barges? Give up? Me, that's who! Was I scared? You bet. Can you read my writing? I'm still shaking and it's been hours.

Pa was pretty tickled, and I guess it felt okay to help out. But don't worry. I'm not planning to join the Navy and come pester you on your ship. Robbie's the one who's planning to do that. And I'm not sure I want to join up for factory work either. A person gets real tired and dirty. Did Ma write and tell you? She's working at the mill. So you see, we're all helping out, one way or another.

Take care of yourself, Jim, and come home as quick as you can. We love you. We miss you.

Your sister,
Charlotte

Charlotte stretched her fingers. It felt good to write to Jim, even if her hands got tired. Red marks from that rope still crisscrossed the palms of her hands. And she hadn't lied to Jim—it was nearly midnight and her insides still felt wobbly.

Jim might not even think it was worth writing about. He probably did worse things, harder and scarier things, every single day in the Navy. Rough water on the Mon, how did that compare to an ocean?

Charlotte closed her eyes and tried to imagine what kind of ship Jim served on. She'd seen plenty of them on the newsreels at the movies—every time a new ship was finished, some movie star in an evening gown broke a bottle over the bow. Just a few miles down the Ohio River, in Ambridge, they were building battleships. Maybe using some of Ma's steel plate. The Navy had even taken over some fancy ocean liners to use for troop ships. Imagine if Jim got to work on one of those. They were so huge, a person wouldn't even feel like she was on the ocean. Wouldn't have to look at the water.

Charlotte felt a shameful heat rush into her cheeks. Here she was sitting at home, safe, and not able to sleep because she was scared of the river. Somewhere, in a huge ocean, her brother braved storms and enemy planes, rough water and torpedoes. Why was she such a coward?

She sighed and looked back over the letter she'd written, checking it. She'd been careful. She hadn't put in anything the censors might snip out, like their town, or the name of the mill, or what Ma was working on. No defense secrets at all.

Then she frowned. She herself had been a censor. She'd left out something important. It wasn't something they would cut out of her letter with their tiny, sharp scissors. But it wasn't a thing Charlotte could admit, even to her brother. Yes, what she'd written was true. She missed him and wanted him to come home safe. But her reasons—they weren't all so good. She scratched a few words on the back of an old arithmetic paper.

Come home, Jim. We miss you. I miss you. I want you back here where you belong so Ma gets that gray look out of her eyes and remembers how to smile again. I miss the old Ma. And it sure would make Pa happy to have you working on the Rose like you used to. And then I wouldn't have to.

Charlotte blinked back tears. How could a person say such a selfish thing? Or even think it? She balled up the paper and threw it into the trash.

CHAPTER 8
DOWN BY THE TRACKS

The next morning, Charlotte had to take Robbie to get his stitches out before school. She had a late-note for Robbie's teacher and one for Mrs. Alexander too. It must have been a morning for notes, for when she reached into her desk for her history book, she found a folded scrap of paper with her name written in careful letters. She opened it quickly.

Meet me at recess! The mystery is solved! Sophie.

Was that possible? Had something happened this morning while she was getting Robbie to the doctor? Charlotte glanced at Betsy and motioned toward Sophie's desk. Betsy shrugged, then turned back to her book.

The morning seemed to go on forever. Finally lunchtime arrived, and after lunch, recess. In the school yard, Charlotte spotted Sophie partly hidden in the shadows of the building, talking to her older sister.

Sophie looked like she was asking for something.

Her sister Helen was shaking her head. Sophie turned and pointed toward Charlotte and Betsy. Helen kept on shaking her head. Finally Sophie snatched something from Helen's pocket and hurried over to where the girls stood.

She pulled on Charlotte's arm. "Come on. Over there in the corner. Where nobody will see." She held something in her hand.

"What is it, Sophie?"

"Charlotte?" Mrs. Alexander's voice came up behind her.

Sophie spun around and quickly stuck her hand into her jacket pocket.

"Charlotte, dear, I came over to ask about your brother's injury, but I seem to have interrupted something. Sophie, what's that in your pocket?"

"Nothing."

Mrs. Alexander held out her hand. "Sophie Jaworski . . ."

Sophie reached into her pocket and pulled out two small squares of stiff paper. She gave them to the teacher, then looked down at her shoes.

"Why . . . whatever is going on? The three of you, follow me."

Next thing Charlotte knew, the girls were upstairs sitting on stools in Mr. Costa's science room. He and Mrs. Alexander were shaking their heads. What had Sophie gotten them into?

"Charlotte Campbell, what's going on?"

"I don't know, ma'am. You got there just when I did."

Her voice quavered. Charlotte wasn't a tattletale, but even if she were, this time she had no idea what Sophie was up to.

"Betsy?"

"Me neither. I don't know what Sophie had."

"What she had is quite clear," Mrs. Alexander said. "Mr. Costa's draft card. And a club membership card. How and why is not clear. Sophie Jaworski, did you take these?"

Sophie shook her head slowly. "No, ma'am. I didn't take anything."

Mr. Costa frowned at them. "Jaworski. You have a sister? Helen? In the eighth grade?"

Sophie nodded, looking more miserable every second.

"Shall we get Helen, or do you want to tell us what happened?" Mrs. Alexander's eyes had turned so dark they looked black.

"I think I know what's going on," the science teacher said. He sighed, then sat behind his desk. "Midmorning sometime, I discovered my wallet lying on the floor next to the windows. I checked it and no money was missing, so I thought I'd somehow dropped it. I hadn't dropped it, though, had I, Sophie?"

She didn't speak, just shook her head and looked sick.

"I don't understand," Mrs. Alexander said.

By now, Charlotte was beginning to. Apparently, so was Mr. Costa. "Your sister and her friends," he began. "They've had their suspicions, haven't they?" He turned to

Mrs. Alexander. "Ever since the metal was taken, the eighth grade has been buzzing like a hive of yellowjackets. Evidently, I'm one of their suspects."

"But why?" Mrs. Alexander looked shocked. "Sophie . . ."

"That—that draft card," Sophie stammered. "Helen says if you have one, it means you're supposed to be in the Army. And you're not. That other card, it says 'Sons of Italy.' Helen says it means you're on the wrong side in the war. With that Mussolini . . ."

Mr. Costa turned toward Sophie, and Charlotte could see how young he was. "Oh, Sophie. I'd hoped I wouldn't have to go into all this. But clearly, there's been some confusion. A draft card simply means a man has registered for the draft. It doesn't mean he can join up."

Mrs. Alexander shot such a ferocious glare at Sophie, it made Charlotte feel the tiniest bit sorry for the girl.

Mr. Costa took a tired breath and went on. "I tried to enlist, you see. I argued and argued with Mr. Butler down at the draft board, but it didn't do any good. They classified me 4-F—unfit for combat." He pointed to a spot on the card. "I had rheumatic fever as a child. It damaged my heart." He put the draft card in his pocket.

"As you now may understand, I can't serve in the Army, much as I'd like to. I'm not a coward or a slacker, just not strong enough. I hope my draft status is clear now, although it would have been much easier just to ask me, wouldn't it?" He lifted the other card and looked at it before he put it in his pocket. "The Sons of Italy is a lodge, sort of like the Elks or the Moose lodges. I joined because my father asked me to. Not because of Mussolini."

"What should we do next?" Mrs. Alexander asked.

"These girls aren't to blame," he said in a quiet voice. "I'll deal with the eighth graders."

Charlotte let out her breath as they walked down the hall. Poor Mr. Costa. He'd been innocent all along. "Sophie Jaworski, I'm never believing another thing you say. You got us into big trouble."

"We're not in trouble, not yet," Betsy said. Her blue eyes had dark circles underneath and she was frowning. "But we will be."

"Why? What's the matter?"

"This morning before school, while you were taking Robbie to the doctor . . ." Betsy hugged herself.

"What?"

"I'll tell you what," Sophie interrupted. "Zalenchak and Merkow came back to school today."

"And?" Charlotte really didn't want to know, but she had a feeling she couldn't escape this one.

"They've challenged Pete and his friends to a fight today, that's what," Betsy said. "Down by the tracks. After school."

Charlotte's stomach turned. A fight wouldn't solve anything. It would just make things worse. For a moment, Charlotte imagined she had some of Pa's heavy line in her hands. Wished she could swing a rope around those mean eighth graders and stop the fight.

But Zalenchak and Merkow weren't like barges. They had minds of their own and they'd steer where they wanted. She couldn't do anything to stop them.

There was an empty place, down near the river and the railroad tracks, where the houses stopped and before the factories started. Once a long row of houses had stood there, with families and kids and dogs filling the street with noise. But years back, one of the houses had caught a spark from the mill and the whole row had burned. Now, only crumbling stone foundations marked where the houses had stood. Nobody wanted to rebuild there, on the chance that another spark might find a roof. So the street was clear for the whole length of a block, and a person could see a fair distance in both directions.

When anybody said a fight *down by the tracks,* they meant that spot. Charlotte knew about it; every kid in school knew, even the little ones. But she hadn't ever gone there and watched before. Sure, she'd walked by, but only when it was empty, a weedy patch with old cracked cement, tumbling-down stones, and a broken bottle or two.

She held tight to her schoolbooks and hurried along, wishing she didn't have to go. She glanced sideways at

Betsy, whose face was pale and stiff-looking. "You sure you want to see this?"

"I don't want to. I have to. Pete's my cousin. He got into this trouble because of me. You don't have to come, Charlotte."

"Of course I do. If I hadn't gotten this dumb idea of collecting scrap, and if we hadn't been so darn good at it, nobody would have stolen anything. So it's my fault too."

"Charlotte—"

"It's true, Bets. People are all fighting and snooping and suspecting each other. I wish we'd never started the drive."

"Too late for that," Betsy said. "Come on. We can stand over there, near the alley. So we won't be in the middle of things."

Other kids were gathering in the alley, and some had climbed onto old foundation stones for a better view. At least half the school had shown up for the fight. A familiar shape brushed past. Charlotte reached out and grabbed Robbie. "What are you doing here, buster?"

"Watching."

"Nope. You get home."

"Will not."

"Come on, Robbie. You could get hurt."

"So could you."

"I don't think they'll punch any girls. But you—"

"They won't mess with little kids either. So, is it true? Is Betsy's cousin going to plaster them?"

Betsy nodded. "That's what Pete says. He's got five of his pals to back him up. Look." She pointed.

Pete Schmidt and five other seventh-grade boys marched down the street and across the tracks. From the other direction, Zalenchak and Merkow and their friends swaggered up.

Betsy grabbed Charlotte's arm. "It's really going to happen."

"There are so many people, I can't see from here." Robbie grumbled and tried to pull loose.

Charlotte held him tight by his belt. "You're sticking with us, buster. I got in enough trouble when you cut your hand. What do you think Ma would do to me if I let some kid crack you in the head? Now be quiet and stop squirming."

Near the tracks, the two lines of boys stepped closer to each other. The onlookers bunched together in tight little knots and stopped whispering. Pete's chin jutted out and his cheeks burned bright red.

Frankie Zalenchak had on the meanest scowl Charlotte had ever seen. And he was bigger than Pete. "Filthy Kraut! Nazi scum!" Frankie yelled.

Pete stepped closer. "Dirty stinking Hunky," he shouted. "Go back to Hungary or wherever you came from. You don't belong here."

"Who's gonna make me leave, huh?" Frankie stuck his chin out. "*You,* pip-squeak?"

Pete hauled back and socked Frankie in the stomach.

Frankie popped him one in the jaw.

After that, it was all grunts and punches and kicks. The other fellas made a circle around the fighters with their hands bunched into fists at their sides. How long until the whole lot of them started pounding on each other? A smell rose in the air, dust and sweat. Charlotte's stomach jumped around.

"Get him, Pete, get him," Robbie yelled.

Charlotte clapped her hand over his mouth. "You hush. You want them coming over here and smacking you?"

He shook his head and she let go, putting her arm around Betsy's waist. She could feel her friend shaking. Or maybe Charlotte was the one shaking.

A car engine sounded from the avenue. One of the boys in the circle turned, then shouted, "Hey, Frankie Z. Hold up, Frank, somebody's coming."

Boys from the circle stepped in and pulled Pete and Frankie apart. But they didn't seem to be looking at the dirty faces and bloody noses. They all turned and stared toward the avenue. Even Frankie and Pete. It was so quiet you could hear the spin of tires on pavement.

Charlotte turned, and what she saw made her breath catch. The brown car from the government. The car every family dreaded.

Frozen in place like the rest, she could only watch and mumble prayers. "Please, please, not my house. Don't stop at my house. Please."

The brown car crossed the tracks and turned onto Talbott Avenue. She hugged Betsy tighter and felt Robbie pull close on her other side.

"No. No. No," she whispered.

One of the boys in the circle crossed himself.

"Keep going. Keep going."

The only thing that moved was the brown car. It rolled slowly down Talbott Avenue, stopping at the cross streets and then starting up again.

Charlotte could tell when the car had passed a boy's street, when his shoulders let down and he could breathe again. But *she* couldn't. Not yet.

"Jim?" Robbie whispered.

"Hush. Don't say it. Don't say anything." She gripped his arm.

She stared down the avenue, and at last the brown car passed by her house and Betsy's and turned up a side street. It parked there, still in sight.

She felt her breath come out, and she drew in fresh, sweet air. She stretched her shoulders, but still she couldn't take her eyes off the street, off the man who was climbing out of the brown car. Now he was shutting the car door, and now, walking around the front and up the steps to the second house in from the corner.

"No! Not Tony. Oh, Ma . . ."

A cry rose from the knot of boys, and they separated. One kid stood alone for a moment rubbing his eyes. Then he dug his heels into the pavement and ran down the avenue, pumping his arms and legs so hard Charlotte could feel sweat rise on her own body.

Every kid watched him run, sorry as could be, except for that one part, the selfish part that was saying thank you. *Thank you for not letting it stop in front of my house.*

Slowly, one at a time, the kids drifted down the avenue. Charlotte held tight to Betsy and Robbie as her feet began to move.

Nobody said anything. Nobody had to. Everybody knew that by tomorrow, Frankie Zalenchak's ma would have a gold star hanging in her front window instead of a blue one.

Chapter 9
A Rocky Cove

When they reached home, Robbie ran for the third floor. Charlotte went to her room and sat on the bed, trying to make her legs stop trembling. She searched among her schoolbooks and papers for her history book, then flipped through until she found her list of suspects. As she read the names, all she could feel was shame. Who was she to accuse these people of stealing?

And what a list she'd made—Paul Rossi, who had brothers fighting; Mr. Costa, who wanted to enlist and couldn't; the school janitor, who'd only been nice to everybody for his whole life; some poor little kid in Robbie's class with a busted lunch pail. And there at the bottom, Zalenchak and Merkow. Seeing Frankie Zalenchak's name on her list was the worst. She tore up the paper and flushed the little pieces down the toilet.

She gathered her books and wandered downstairs to

the kitchen, wishing hard that today of all days Ma could be home. But she wasn't. She'd made a noodle casserole for supper, and Charlotte was supposed to put it in to heat. She did that, then settled at the kitchen table to do her homework. But no matter how many times she stared at the fractions in her arithmetic book, all she could see was the brown car. All she could hear was Frankie Zalenchak's voice crying out, "No! Not Tony."

She stood and paced around the house, then stopped by the front window to touch the points of Jim's blue star. *Could have been me,* she thought. *Could have been Robbie and me, or Betsy or anybody. We've all got brothers.*

Ma had heard about Frankie's brother at the mill. When she walked in the door, grimy as she was, she grabbed onto Charlotte and hugged her so hard it hurt. "You heard?"

Charlotte nodded. "We saw the brown car come. I was afraid—"

"Oh, honey, this is so hard." Ma buried her face in Charlotte's hair.

"I hate it, Ma. I want it all to just go away. I want to close my eyes, and when I open them again, it will all be over—the war and the fighting and the ships going down and that brown car . . ."

"I know, honey, I know. We all want that. But . . ."

They stood holding on to each other for a long time, then Ma seemed to straighten herself. "I'm going to take my bath. Will you set the table? Your pa should be home soon."

Pa came home wearing a stern face, but carrying two bundles. He set one at Robbie's place and one at Charlotte's. "I bought these this morning to celebrate my brave crew of yesterday," he began. "Maybe after supper . . ."

When they sat to eat, nobody seemed very hungry. Robbie's eyes were puffy and red, and so were Ma's. Charlotte couldn't tell if she'd scorched the casserole or if the odd taste in her mouth came from seeing the brown car. Somehow they managed to eat part of the meal, and after a while, they began to talk, about ordinary things.

"I've got a long haul coming," Pa said. "One of the big tugs is down for repair, and they need me to tow coal in from a mine down in Fayette County. I'll be gone most of the week. Will you be all right?"

Ma shook her head. "Seems like everything goes wrong at once. Somebody's sick at the mill and they asked me to cover the swing shift for the rest of the week. Charlotte, can you manage here alone from four until midnight? I could get somebody to stay, but . . ."

"She won't be alone," Robbie said. "I'll be here too. We aren't babies."

"We'll be fine, Ma," Charlotte said. "Betsy's right next door. Her ma will help if we need anything."

Ma patted Charlotte's hand. "Thanks, honey. In spite of everything, we do have to keep going."

Then Pa pointed to the packages. "I know this is a bad night. With a war on, we'll have some bad nights, no hiding from that. We've all got to hang on to each other to make it through the rough spots. But yesterday was a good day. I was very proud of both of you. So today I stopped by the store and . . . well, open them up."

Robbie smiled a little as he lifted the box lid. He held up a white shirt with a square collar and a tie in the front. A boy-size Navy shirt. "Neat, Pa. It's like Jim's. Can I put it on right now?"

"Let Charlotte open hers first," Ma said.

Charlotte slipped her box open. Inside, she saw tan cloth—a jacket with wide lapels and buttons. Underneath, she found a matching skirt. "Oh, Pa. It's a WAC suit? Really?" It was like a woman's Army uniform, but in her size. The Cussick twins had worn suits just like this to school last week, and Sophie Jaworski had bragged that her ma was buying one too. Last week Charlotte would have loved the suit, loved the chance to wear it before Sophie got one. But now it just made the war seem closer.

"Thanks, Pa," she whispered. "It's really swell."

Pa nodded. "I'll understand if you want to wait a few days . . ."

After supper was finally over and the kitchen clean, Charlotte sat in her room to study for a history test. The WAC uniform hung on the doorknob, sturdy and serious. A knock came at the door.

"Charlie, can I come in? It's important."

"Sure, Robbie." She set her book aside.

He stepped into her room, wearing his sailor shirt. He'd tied a square knot in the front, but it was crooked.

"You want me to fix that?"

"I guess." He stood and fidgeted while she straightened the knot.

"There. You look like a real sailor," she said.

He frowned at her, then took a deep breath. "I didn't really come about shirts or knots, Charlie. We have to go get more scrap, right away. I got my stitches out now."

"Ma doesn't want us collecting scrap," Charlotte warned.

"Ma doesn't have to know. Come on, Charlie. It's important. If we keep on collecting metal, maybe they can make a ship or a plane with it. So we can beat the Japs and the Germans. So Jim doesn't . . . you know." He wouldn't look at her.

"The brown car?"

He nodded and sat next to her on the bed. He swung his legs. "We gotta do something, Charlie. We can't just sit around. If you won't help, I'll do it by myself."

"You'll do what by yourself?"

"Promise not to tell."

"I won't."

"Okay. You know that pile of metal we saw from the *Rose*? I want to get it and take it to school."

Charlotte's stomach tightened. "It was steep there. We'll never find that junk from the riverbank."

"So what? We'll find it from the water then. Unless

you're too scared. Unless you're such a chicken you'd rather sit home than help win this war."

Charlotte winced. Was she a chicken? She didn't like the river, that wasn't news. But she had helped Pa rope in those barges. So maybe she could at least try to find the metal. "How about looking from the bank first? After school tomorrow? We'll ask Betsy to come along."

"And your friend Paul. I like that guy," Robbie said. "He knows about stitches and shots. Besides, he carried me—imagine how much junk he can lift."

"I guess," Charlotte said. "With Ma working the swing shift and Pa on a long haul, we could spend a while there. But don't wear your new shirt unless you want Ma to figure out what we're up to."

Robbie saluted. "Aye, aye. Top secret. No uniforms." He raced from her room and she heard his footsteps thumping up to the third floor.

As she stood to close her door, she ran her hand along the shoulder of the WAC uniform. In her mind, she heard again the voice of the President, calling for sacrifice on the home front.

"It is for them. It is for us. It is for victory."

But how much will victory cost, she wondered. How many more brown cars?

❧

"We can't go down there. It's too steep," Charlotte said the next day after school. They'd trudged along the railroad tracks into North Braddock—upriver, past the mill, past the railroad bridge. Here the banks narrowed, with weeds and small trees clinging to the slope, a tumble of pale spring greens and golds. Instead of flats with houses, massive piles of limestone boulders guarded the water's edge. On the other side, a rocky hill seemed to climb straight out of the muddy Mon. She peered down through overgrown bushes toward the river, holding tight to a small tree so she wouldn't slip.

"But, Charlie, there's so much good stuff down there. And it's ours, if we just climb down and—"

"And what, buster? Get your other hand torn up? What do you want, a matched set? We aren't going down."

Betsy gave Charlotte a hand and pulled her up higher where the bank flattened out. "Can't we do anything? There *is* a lot of metal down there. You can see it shine in the sun."

Robbie grinned at Betsy, like she'd taken his side. "Yeah, Charlie. Can't we? Not everybody is a scaredy-cat. How about it, Paul?"

Paul Rossi had been standing to the side, studying the rocky wall that dropped down toward the river. He looked up when Robbie mentioned his name. "Your sister's right. We can't climb down this, and even if we could, we'd never be able to carry the stuff out. It's too steep."

"So it's a dead end?" Charlotte sighed. Partly she was

relieved, but there *was* a lot of scrap down there, metal for bombs or bullets.

Paul shook his head. "I didn't say it was a dead end. I just said we couldn't climb down. No reason we can't get in there with a boat."

"If we had a boat," Betsy said. "Charlotte's father has a tug, but he's away all week."

"We don't need a tug," Paul said. "I got a rowboat at home. Belongs to my brothers, but they'd let me use it. Especially for this."

"But—" Charlotte began.

"Great! I knew we could do it!" Robbie shouted. "Let's go right now."

"Wait a minute," Charlotte said.

"Come on. Nobody's home. We won't get in trouble. I'm going with Paul, even if you aren't. So there."

"I can't go," Betsy said. "I promised my mother I'd get home in time to help with supper. I've got to hurry now or she'll holler."

"Fine," Robbie snapped. "You dumb girls just go home then. Me and Paul can—"

"Watch it, Robbie," Paul said. "Betsy can't help it if her ma's expecting her home." He looked at Charlotte, and she saw a challenge in his eyes.

"I'll come," she said.

After Betsy left for home, Charlotte and Robbie followed Paul to his house. From a shed back in the alley, he hauled out a rowboat on a small wheeled trailer. Then he tossed in a pair of fishing poles.

"We're not going fishing," Robbie said. "How come you're taking poles?"

Charlotte wondered the same thing, but she was glad Robbie'd been the one to ask.

"Never hurts to have fishing stuff along," Paul said. He tugged on the trailer and pulled the boat toward the water. "Gives us a good excuse to be on the river. Before they went off to the war, my brothers used to row up and down near the banks and watch for girls. But they kept their fishing gear out so nobody would know what they were up to."

"Girls? That's dumb," Robbie said. "I'd rather catch fish. Even catfish are better than girls."

Charlotte grinned. She pushed the rowboat from behind as they neared the tracks. The sun behind her sat low in the sky. The Rankin Bridge cast long, rippling shadows on the water, but it was still light enough that she could see to ease the rowboat into the river without slipping.

Paul held a rope by the bow. "Go ahead, climb in. I'll steady the boat."

"Where are the life jackets?" Charlotte asked.

"Life jackets? To go rowing on the Monongahela? We'll stay close to the banks, I promise. Come on."

Charlotte climbed in and the little boat rocked from side to side. When Robbie stepped in, she leaned hard to balance his weight. Little boats were so tippy. Compared to this tub, the *Rose* was an ocean liner.

Paul stepped aboard smoothly and took up the oars. He rowed close to shore as he'd promised, and soon they were making good time against the current. "Get out your fishing poles," he said. "And try to look like you know what you're doing."

A large working boat passed them in the middle of the channel, sending out a hefty wake. The rowboat rocked and Charlotte's stomach rocked right along with it. She dropped a line in the water. She knew how to fish, but she was used to a bigger boat.

As they headed upriver, the sun sank lower, turning the sky and the water around them pale pink. Paul pulled closer to the shoreline, into a small cove. "About here, don't you think?"

Robbie shifted so he could see the bank, and then leaned out, nearly sending Charlotte overboard. "Yeah. I see the stuff. There's a whole pile there. Boy oh boy! I'm gonna—"

"You're gonna sit tight, buster," Charlotte growled. "Otherwise you'll get us all wet. Wait till Paul pulls the boat in before you start jumping around."

Paul shoved on the oars and the boat scraped along the river bottom. Robbie hopped out with a splash and yanked on the rope, pulling the nose of the boat onto shore. Charlotte climbed out carefully, glad for solid ground underfoot. When Paul climbed out, he beached the boat and looped the rope around a low-hanging tree.

Robbie ran ahead toward the stash of metal. "Oh, wow! Look at this. So much stuff!"

By the time Charlotte caught up to him, he was climbing over the junk. "Watch out," she ordered. "If you're not careful, you'll get cut again or twist an ankle, and it's a lot harder to get to the doctor's office from here."

"But, Charlie—"

"Listen to your sister," Paul said. "You don't want another shot, do you?"

"No, but look. Right up here. I collected this baby buggy once before. Look, Charlie, it's the exact same one."

"Come on, Robbie. You're nuts."

"It *is* the same. Look." He yanked hard and some of the metal came loose from the pile.

"What's he talking about, Charlotte?" Paul asked.

"We cleaned out an old lady's backyard and cellar for the scrap drive. He thinks he recognizes junk from her place."

"Is it possible? If it's the same baby buggy . . . that means . . ."

Charlotte's breath caught. "It means we've found the thief's hiding place," she whispered. "That's halfway to catching him. Let me see that buggy, Robbie."

She climbed up to where she could reach the old buggy. With Robbie and Charlotte each holding up one end, they picked their way down the pile of junk and set the frame on flat, damp ground.

"Look, it's gray cloth, just like the one we found in Mrs. Dubner's cellar." Robbie shoved the frame. Like before, three wheels worked, but one stuck. The left rear one.

"Is it the same?" Paul asked.

"You bet," Robbie said.

"Charlotte?"

"I . . . I think so. The color matches, and the stuck wheel. The one we found had a rough, rusty place under the handle, on the right side."

Paul studied the handle. "Right here? Like this?"

Charlotte ran her fingers along the bar. On the right side something snagged her fingertips. She looked underneath and found a circular patch of rust. "We found it, then. The thief's hiding place."

"What should we do next, Charlotte? What do you think?" Paul had a serious look on his face.

She scanned the bank on both sides of the junk pile. Then she rubbed her arms to chase away a sudden chill. "I think we should get out of here. Right away, before he comes back."

CHAPTER 10

NIGHT FISHING

I say we go back after supper tonight and watch for the thief," Paul began. "We know to be careful now. With three of us, we'll be all right." He'd beached his rowboat near his house and was tipping it on one side to dump out any water.

"I don't know," Charlotte said. "What if there are three of *them*? Or five? There's so much metal there, you'd need an army to carry it all."

"You're just being chicken again," Robbie said. "If Jim were home, he'd come."

"Make sense, Robbie. If Jim were home, there wouldn't be a war on and we wouldn't be collecting all this junk in the first place." She sighed.

"What do *you* think we should do, Charlotte?" Paul asked.

"How about telling the police? Wouldn't they be better at catching the thief? We could tell them where to look."

"Yeah," Robbie said. "They could set up a trap, like in the movies."

Paul shook his head. "Do you think they'd bother with a pile of junk? They don't have enough men for their regular work these days. They'd call this kid stuff. They'd laugh."

"Maybe." Charlotte frowned. If Paul was right, then the three of them had to catch the thief. Or thieves. "Okay, *if* we go back and keep watch, I'd like to figure things out better first. So we know what we're looking for."

Robbie rolled his eyes at her. "Come on, Charlie, we're looking for a thief. You know that."

"Okay, Mr. Smarty-Pants." Charlotte shook her head. "What I'd like to know is *why* the thief took the stuff. And how he knew about it in the first place. That might tell us what kind of thief we're trying to catch. If it's some robber gang with knives or guns, I'm not going near the place."

"But, Charlie—"

Paul tipped his head to one side. "Your sister's right," he said. "If we think things through, try to put ourselves in the criminal's mind . . ."

A shiver went up Charlotte's back. She couldn't help remembering all those newspaper articles Paul brought to school. "You can think like a criminal if you want, but I'm not going to."

"I bet you already have, without knowing it," he said. "Good cops do it all the time. I know, 'cause I'm going to be a cop one of these days."

"Really? Is that why you're always collecting crime stories?" Charlotte began.

Paul shook his head at her. "That's my business. Right now, we've got a thief to catch. I bet you've already figured out how he knew about the metal. Haven't you?"

Charlotte looked at him, puzzled.

"It just makes sense that he's connected to the school," Paul said. "He must go there, or work there, or something. He knows about the metal because he's there. And if he's not a stranger, nobody gets suspicious."

Charlotte thought about Paul's words. She *had* known that, maybe not in words, but inside. Most of the people on her old suspects list were connected to the school. A shadow flitted across her mind. Mr. Willis. No, absolutely not. She wouldn't think that about a nice old man who was kind to everybody. "Okay, but why? Why take all that junk?"

"He's mean, that's why," Robbie said. He picked up a stick and smacked it against the rowboat. "I want to catch him and pop him one, right in the kisser."

"I don't think that's the reason," Paul said. "I've been trying to figure it out all along. There's only one reason a person would take the stuff. He's planning to sell it. He needs the money."

Charlotte shook her head. "Swell—that helps a lot. Who wouldn't like a pile of free money? Last time I looked, Braddock wasn't exactly swimming in millionaires."

Paul looked at her like she was Robbie's age. "There's a difference between wanting money and needing it. Sure, most people would like extra moolah. Who wouldn't like to find a ten-spot on the sidewalk?"

"Think of all the candy bars you could buy." Robbie patted his stomach and grinned.

"Shh. Go on, Paul."

"It's simple. With the war on, most people are working hard. Bringing in good money. So they're doing okay. If a family has boys in the service, they get an allotment every month too. My ma does."

"So?" Where was he going with all this?

"Taking that metal is like stealing from the war. A person would have to be pretty desperate. Flat-out broke, if you ask me."

Charlotte rubbed her forehead. "If you're right, that's all the more reason we should tell the police and stay away. If the thief's a desperate person—"

"Aaack!" Robbie grabbed his own neck with his hands and made nasty, choking sounds.

"Desperate poor, not desperate mean," Paul said. He scowled at Robbie. "There's a difference, believe me."

The way he said it gave Charlotte a creepy feeling, like Paul might know what it was like to be that poor. She needed to change the subject right away.

"I still don't want to sit there in a little rowboat and watch for the crook," she began. "But maybe I'd do it if there were some way to hide. If we could watch without being spotted . . ."

"We can do that," Robbie said. "Easy as pie. All we've got to do is row up there at night. Once it's dark, nobody will see us. Of course, we'll have to wear dark clothes and sneak around and not talk, but we can do that."

"Ridiculous," Charlotte began.

"Swell," Paul said at the same moment. "We'll take along the fishing gear, just in case."

Robbie grinned. Paul punched his shoulder. And Charlotte's stomach began to tie itself in knots.

On the river? In a rowboat? At night? She'd never survive it.

The sky had turned a deep bluish gray by the time Charlotte and Robbie rejoined Paul beside the river. Full darkness would come in a half hour, and they'd need that time to get themselves into position.

Charlotte carried a bag of supplies—some cheese and crackers, a jar of water, a flashlight, a sweater. In the other hand she held Jim's baseball bat, and slung over her shoulder, a life jacket. "I can't believe I let you two talk me into this," she grumbled. She'd tried to get Betsy to come along, but with no success.

"Come on, Charlie, get in the boat," Robbie said.

"I can't wait to get started. It's a real spy mission."

"Real spies are quiet," Paul reminded him. "Get all your gabbing done before we reach that cove."

"Roger, capt'n."

Paul reached out and messed Robbie's hair, just like Jim always did. Charlotte had to bite down on her bottom lip to keep from crying. *Don't think of him now,* she scolded herself. But wait—Jim was the exact person she ought to think about. He was a sailor. He was good with boats. And he was brave. So maybe if she thought about him, some of his courage might rub off. And besides, this hunt for the thief, the scrap drive, all of it—if it wasn't for Jim, who was it for?

Paul settled into the rowboat and dipped his oars. Charlotte felt the current surge and push against them. It seemed stronger somehow than it had in the afternoon. Along the bank, trees and bushes became shadow creatures with long arms and sharp claws.

Robbie leaned forward in the boat and pointed upstream. "Look, Charlie, the sky. It's like the Fourth of July."

In the distance, she could see the mill chimneys— skinny, shadowy pipes that blasted the darkening sky with red and orange flame. On flat land beside the chimneys, slag heaps burned like yellow-gold mountains. As Charlotte stared, a huge ladle poured a stream of liquid fire from furnace to mold. Steel, running like water but so hot that just the fumes could scorch a person's lungs. Ma was in there, in that mill, working a crane near those furnaces. It was nearly as scary as being on the river.

"Shh. We're getting close. I'll row upstream a ways and let her drift back so we can watch the whole cove. But we'll stay away from the bank so if he comes, he won't see us."

"Right, Paul," Charlotte said. "And so we can escape if there are a bunch of them."

"Chicken," Robbie whispered.

"Shh."

That was the last talking anybody did. Paul had the boat pointed upstream, and every once in a while he'd row a few strokes beyond the bend in the river and then let the current carry them back.

Charlotte focused her eyes on the dark riverbank. When she'd looked at the mill chimneys, the flaming sky had taken away some of her night sight. So she kept her eyes down—down where she had to look at the black water rippling past, carrying them backward. The water reminded her of black velvet, except that velvet was soft and warm and comforting. The Mon was harsh and cold and threatening, even on a May night. A train whistle blew, and downstream a tug's whistle answered. She pulled her sweater from her bag and slipped it on.

As she was buttoning it, she heard a voice—no, two voices, raised in an argument. She reached out to touch Robbie's hand. In the dark, she could see his face nodding. He'd heard it too. She strained to listen. It sounded like a man and a child.

"I don't want to," the child said.

"What you want don't matter. You'll do as I say."

"But—"

"No buts," the man's voice said.

Charlotte fisted her hands and felt her fingernails bite into her palms. Were these their thieves? She ran a finger along the handle of Jim's baseball bat. Would she dare swing it?

"Please don't make me," the child's voice continued. Charlotte heard sniffs; the poor kid was crying. And then a slap and the rough sound of a person hauling somebody where he didn't want to go.

She turned and caught Paul's eye. He shook his head. He was staring at the riverbank just like she'd been. Neither of them had seen a thing.

The boat rocked slightly, and Charlotte felt Robbie creep back from the bow to sit close beside her. Noiselessly, she slid over to make room. Little brother or not, he was a comfort. His hand reached out for hers, and it was cold and shaking. Were those voices coming toward them?

Except for the regular lapping of the river against the rowboat, she hadn't heard any water sounds. So if the crooks were coming, it had to be by land. But even as Paul drew the boat closer to shore, nothing moved, nothing showed in the bend of the river but the shine of water, the bare branches of trees, and the misshapen shadows that outlined the scrap pile.

Minutes went by—fifteen, maybe twenty—and still nothing happened. Paul kept rowing upstream to keep the cove in view, but except for that, nothing moved.

Then a splash. And another, coming toward them from the middle of the river. Whatever it was, it sounded big. Charlotte grabbed her flashlight in one hand, the bat in the other. She waited, counting her breaths. The splashing got closer.

From behind, Paul nudged her. She shoved the flashlight into Robbie's hands and gripped the bat with both of hers. She elbowed Robbie's side and he switched on the light, pointing it toward the sounds.

"Oh, geez. A dumb mutt." Paul's voice came out shaky.

Charlotte released the bat and stared where the light pointed. A shaggy, good-sized dog was swimming across the water toward them. He looked almost like he was trying to wag his tail.

"If we don't watch out, that dog will try to climb in this rowboat and dump us all out," she said. "Let's go home. I've had enough excitement for one night."

Robbie's voice chimed in, "Me too. I'm kinda cold."

Then she heard herself saying, "Well, smarten up, buster. Tomorrow night wear a sweater."

Had she really done that? Had she somehow agreed to come out here again? She looked out on the river and shivered. Where had those voices come from?

Chapter 11
Voices in the Fog

The next morning, Charlotte awoke to a gray and rainy sky. Thank heavens, they wouldn't have to go out on the river today. Only a crazy person would do that. As she dressed for school, she peered out the window. A steady rain, the kind that could go on all day. *Good for the garden,* she thought. *And good for me.*

She needed a gentle day and evening. After last night's hours on the river, she'd stayed awake a long time, afraid to let herself drift off to sleep. And when she finally did sleep, the dream came again—Jim and the water and the ship, but this time with ghostly voices floating in the mist.

It took the whole walk to school to fill Betsy in on the night's adventures. At school, the rain clouds had cast shadows on everyone. Nobody could remember how to smile. Of course, it didn't help that Frankie Zalenchak came back to school after his brother's funeral. Everywhere

Frankie walked, silence followed. Even when he wasn't nearby, Charlotte didn't dare laugh, because what if he happened to turn the corner and she was laughing? If you had a dead brother, could you ever stand the sound of kids laughing?

By lunchtime, Charlotte felt as stretched and thin as a rubber band on a package. If anybody did or said one more bad thing . . .

"Hey, Charlotte, guess what?" Sophie Jaworski stood with her arms folded across her chest and grinned.

Charlotte had the feeling Sophie might just say that one bad thing. "Not right now, Sophie. I've got to go check with Betsy about something."

"I'll come too," Sophie offered. "That way I can tell you both at the same time." She tagged along like a stray puppy, reminding Charlotte of the dog they'd seen in the river. She shivered at the thought.

When they reached Betsy, Sophie began to talk right away. "We know who the thief is," she began.

"Oh, come on." Charlotte snapped her mouth shut before she said any more, but inside, questions pushed so hard she had to clench her jaw to keep from spitting them out. *What do you know, and how? Did you find the thief's hiding place? No. Did you lurk in the shadows in a puny little rowboat to watch for him? No. Can you do anything at all, besides flap your tongue?*

"Who is it?" Betsy asked.

"Wagon Willie. We know for sure."

Charlotte felt her lungs swell. She took in a huge breath, then another. Her cheeks burned and she made her hands into fists. "That's the dumbest thing I've ever heard, Sophie Jaworski. Take it back."

"I will not. It's true."

"How do you know?"

"He's got keys to the school. By the second time the thief came, there was a lock on the cellar door, remember? So the room was locked up tight. But the thief didn't break the lock to get in. Which means he must have had keys. Wagon Willie has keys. So he's got to be the thief."

"I don't know, Sophie," Betsy began. "Mr. Willis doesn't seem like a bad man."

"Betsy, you should be glad it's him. That way, kids will stop blaming you. You should help prove he did it, don't you see?"

"No." The word came out so hard it nearly burned Charlotte's tongue. "What if somebody else has keys? What if somebody swiped his keys? What if he forgot to lock up that night? What if he put the lock in wrong and it didn't work? What if—"

"Why do you care, Charlotte?" Sophie interrupted. "He's just a crazy old man. My sister says they shouldn't let people like that work in schools. He could scare kids."

"Your sister also said Mr. Costa was an Italian spy," Charlotte said. "When it comes to meanness, your sister's a hundred times more scary than Mr. Willis. And so are you." She grabbed Betsy's arm and marched away from Sophie, who for once had nothing more to say.

They held recess in the gym because of the rain. Charlotte grabbed a jump rope and spun it, jumping as fast as she could. She didn't even count the jumps, her mind was so stirred up. Rumors, suspicion, finger-pointing— it was rotten to think about poor Mr. Willis like that. It made Charlotte furious.

But by the end of recess, his name was a hum, spreading around the room under the sound of jumps and bounces and yells.

Charlotte wanted to stick her fingers in her ears. "What are we going to do, Betsy? Poor Mr. Willis."

"Are you sure he didn't do it?" Betsy replied. "I mean, he could have taken the scrap upriver as easy as anybody else, couldn't he?"

"Not you too!" Charlotte turned away and bumped into Paul Rossi, who was charging toward her with a frown on his face.

"You hear what they're saying? About Wagon Willie?"

"Yeah." Charlotte nodded.

"So what are we going to do about it, Charlotte? Unless you think, like the rest of these bozos, that Mr. Willis has a criminal mind just because he can't talk real smooth."

"I don't think that! But what can we do?"

"Catch the real thief."

Charlotte shook her head. "You don't mean . . . Not tonight . . . Not in the rain . . ."

"Why not? It's a perfect night for a thief. He can come and haul his loot away and nobody will see. Who else would be out?" He grinned at her.

Charlotte swallowed hard. She turned. "Betsy? Can you come?" Betsy understood how she felt about the river. With Betsy in the boat, she might make it through another night on the water. "Please."

"I'd help if I could, Charlotte. You know that. But my ma is so strict."

"But the rain . . ." Charlotte protested, turning back to Paul.

"Come on, Charlotte, your pa's a river man. You've got old oilskins around the house. If not, we've got extras from my brothers. Besides, it's May. A little spring rain never hurt anyone."

Right, Charlotte thought. Spring rain was soft and gentle. Spring rain fed the flowers. But it also fed creeks and rivers. It turned into river water and popped huge barges from their moorings and set them adrift.

"Decide, Charlotte. We have to catch the real thief, or Wagon Willie could be in a lot of trouble. He could lose his job. Unless that doesn't matter to you."

"Of course it matters, but—"

"Great," he said, smacking her shoulder. "Meet me by the boat then. Same time as last night."

༒

"Come on, Charlie. Hurry up. It's getting dark." Robbie stood by the back door, wrapped in one of Pa's old jackets. He kicked at the bottom of the door.

Charlotte buttoned her sweater. "Don't hurry me, buster. I don't want to go at all, so don't push."

"Fine. Me and Paul will do better without you." He reached for the doorknob.

She knocked his hand away. "Let me finish getting dressed. Are you sure you're wrapped up enough?"

"Stop fussing, Charlie. You're worse than Ma."

"Yeah, and how am I supposed to explain to Ma if your clothes get soaked? Should I tell her you took a bath with your pants on?"

"We've been over this already. If anything gets wet, we hide it in Jim's closet. Come on. Paul will leave without us."

Charlotte tightened Jim's spare oilskin around herself. She checked her bag from the night before and picked up the baseball bat. "Okay. I'm ready."

What a lie that was. She'd take ten spelling tests, twenty arithmetic tests, if it meant she didn't have to go out on the water tonight with all that rain. But when she thought about poor Mr. Willis, what choice did she have? She'd spent the afternoon trying to think of a better way to catch the thief and she'd come up empty. Even if they showed the police the stash of metal, somebody could still say Mr. Willis had taken it and hidden it by the river.

She stood on the back porch and locked the door, wishing that somehow Betsy could sneak out and join them.

Robbie bounced down the steps. "Hurry up. I think tonight's the night. I got a feeling about it." He splashed through a puddle and onto the street.

She hurried to catch up. "So do I, buster. A bad feeling."

Her worry didn't lighten when they reached the river. Even in the near-darkness, she could see how angry and muddy it looked. When she stepped into the rowboat, the current rocked her. "Water's high, Paul."

"I know. We'll have to be extra careful. You too, Robbie."

"Aye, aye. Let's go get the crooks."

Paul rowed. The beat of rain on the water hid their slight splashes as the boat nosed into the river. When he pulled his oars out between strokes, the current shoved the boat backward. Staying even with the cove would be hard work tonight. Charlotte might have to take a turn at the oars.

She peered forward into the gloom. If she were rowing, she wouldn't have to look out at the water rushing past. She'd be working too hard to hear it slap against the sides of the boat. She closed her eyes. They hadn't reached the cove yet. She didn't have to look at all. But not seeing was worse, for she could imagine . . .

"Paul. When we get there tonight, could we tie up somewhere? I don't like the feel of the river."

"Maybe. But it would make a getaway harder. I'm not sure which is worse."

Charlotte sighed and huddled on the seat. Already rain was leaking in around her collar and at the tops of her boots. She hugged herself and tried not to shiver. "Maybe we should just wait till Pa comes home and haul the metal to the scrap yard on his tug. Forget about the thief."

"If we don't catch him before your pa comes home, maybe. But tonight we've got to keep watch for the thief. It's a perfect night."

"Perfectly awful," Charlotte grumbled.

"What if they have a motor?" Robbie asked. "We'll never catch them if they have a motor."

"With gas shortages? Not likely," Paul said.

"They could too have a motor," Robbie argued. "If they could steal our metal, they could steal somebody's gas. So there."

"Come on, buster. We've got to be quiet, remember?"

As they neared the small cove, the night grew darker, and fog began to drift along the river, mixing with the rain. Upstream somewhere a train whistle blew, long and loud and so lonesome Charlotte wanted to cry. "We should go home," she said softly. "It's nuts to be out here tonight."

"Shh," Paul warned. "Watch the bank now. I'm going in closer."

Closer meant shallower water. That made Charlotte feel a little better, but in a cove the currents sometimes acted funny. And with fog coming down, a boat could get lost just a few feet from shore.

"Do you see anything, Charlie?" Robbie whispered. "I don't."

"I can barely see the bank. Paul, we really should go home. We won't catch anybody if we can't see."

"I'll tie up then," he said. "We'll use our ears."

As he finished speaking, a low wail blasted the air around them. A tug in midriver. The sound came three times. Charlotte braced herself for the wake. It hit them broadside, knocking the rowboat sideways toward the bank and sloshing water in over their feet.

When the river calmed, Paul rowed toward an overhanging tree. "We'll tie up here. If we can't see the crook, he can't see us. So we'll be fine."

"I'm not sitting in this boat," Charlotte said. "I want solid ground under my feet."

"Come on, Charlie. Don't turn chicken again. The banks are all mud anyway."

"I'll find a rock to sit on." She climbed out, carrying the bat and her bag of supplies.

"Shh," Paul warned again. "Sounds can carry a long way on the water."

Like last night, Charlotte thought. Were that man and child going to come back? Were they mixed up in the stealing? She squinted, trying to spot a protected place to sit. There didn't seem to be any flat rocks nearby, but she found a beached log that was better than mud. She sat, wishing for a thick umbrella of pine branches overhead. But no big trees grew this close to the river, so the rain trickled down her neck.

Minutes crept by, then a half hour. Another train blew. The chuffing of wheels grew loud, then soft, finally disappearing into the fog. "How long?" she whispered. "It's really bad out here."

"Another hour?" Paul said.

"Half? Please?"

"Okay, half."

"Aw, Charlie—"

"Shh. I hear something," Paul whispered.

Charlotte held her breath. Footsteps? The splash of water against a boat? She listened hard over the river noise and the rain.

"It's too hard. I can't bear it, Johnny." A woman's voice.

"I know. I know. But I got no choice." A man.

Robbie slipped out of the boat and crawled next to her on the log. She threw her arm around him. These people didn't sound like thieves, but they sure sounded spooky. They had to be mighty desperate to be out on such a night. And where were they? On the river? On the bank? Charlotte listened for boat sounds but didn't hear any. Just sad voices.

"Do you have to? If you love me . . ."

"I have to. Because I love you. What kind of man would I be if I didn't?"

Charlotte pulled Robbie closer. She heard no more talking, but there was a sound, soft crying, like a kitten would make. They weren't supposed to be hearing this. Nobody was. It felt all wrong.

"Paul. I want to go home. Now." She opened her bag and pulled out the flashlight. Turning sideways to keep any stray light from reaching the river, she flicked on the flashlight, checked her watch quickly, then switched off the light. "We've been out here for more than an hour. The next dry night I'll come back, I promise."

"Shh." His warning came as a soft hiss, barely reaching her ears.

What had he heard or imagined this time? Charlotte held her breath and listened, so hard she could hear her own heart beating and Robbie's soft breathing next to her. Then she heard it too, upstream. The scrape of wood against rock. A splash and the gentle thwack of a rope being tossed to shore.

CHAPTER 12

AT WHISPER BEND

Charlotte froze. She felt Robbie's hand inch over onto her arm, and he dug his nails in, like a kitten will when it's scared. His fingers crept down until they reached her right hand. He tugged on the flashlight she still held. His motion thawed her muscles.

She passed him the flashlight with her right thumb covering the switch, protecting it. With her left palm she covered the end with the lightbulb, then shook her head as if to say, *Don't turn it on yet.* She prayed he understood.

He nodded and she released it into his hands. Bending slowly, she reached for the baseball bat and wrapped both her hands around it.

Upstream, a thump and footsteps.

She peered into the darkness, trying to see Paul's face, but he was too far away, a pale blur in the rainy night.

The footsteps came closer. Was it just one person?

Robbie poked her side with his elbow.

She shook her head. Not yet, not until the thief was close enough to catch. She lifted the bat from the ground and set it on her right shoulder. She glanced toward Paul again and saw motion. She wasn't sure what he was up to.

A twig snapped, so close she could almost feel the bark splinter. She tightened her grip on the bat and prepared to stand. She nudged Robbie.

He flicked on the light.

"Stop right there!" she shouted.

Paul leapt from the rowboat with an oar, ready to swing it.

The light wobbled, then Robbie caught a face in its beam. A boy, or a young man. Dark clothes. A cap. His mouth open, his eyes wide. Then a deep voice. "Oh, geez. No!"

"Don't you move," Robbie warned.

Paul slipped behind the guy. "Not unless you want a taste of this," he shouted, slapping his oar against the water.

Charlotte stood and stepped closer. He was a boy, but older. Jim's age maybe, his size. She could see shadows of a beard on his jaw. Dark hair and dark eyes.

"Joey? Joey, what's happening?" A voice from upstream, from the darkness. A kid's voice.

"Hush. Stay in the boat." He turned to Charlotte and let out a sigh. "It's me you want, not them. They didn't do anything."

"Did you steal our metal?" Robbie demanded.

"Joey, I'm coming to help," the kid called again.

"No! Stay back!"

Noises from upstream, splashes and voices. Then running feet. Two kids burst from the bushes and grabbed Paul's legs from behind.

The thief turned and tugged on them, freeing Paul. "I said not to," he began.

Robbie shined his flashlight on the kids. "I told you, Charlie. I told you it was Tommy Stankowski."

The boy in the light blinked, scowled, and stuck out his jaw. The other kid, a little girl, started to cry.

"Give me that light," Charlotte said. She set down her bat in Paul's boat and took the flashlight from Robbie. She fumbled, then flicked off the switch. "What do we do now?" she asked Paul.

"Take them to the cops," Robbie said.

"Please. I can explain. Just hear me out," the guy said. He threw an arm around each of the kids.

Paul stepped closer and Charlotte watched him study the three thieves. "I think we should hear what he has to say. We can always take him to the cops after. Go on."

"It could take a while," Joey said. "But the little fella is right. I'm Joseph Stankowski. This here's my brother Tommy and my sister Tessa. They didn't do none of this." He pointed to the metal.

"But, Charlie—" Robbie began.

A voice from the bank cut him off. "N-nobody move!"

A powerful glare hit Charlotte in the eyes, blinding her. She raised her hand as a shield. "Who is it?" Was there another thief?

Nobody moved. Charlotte heard scrambling sounds, branches breaking, boots hitting rocks with loud thuds. And then she found herself looking right into a familiar face. "Mr. Willis? What are you doing here?"

"M-m-missy. Shame." He shook his head at her, angry.

She touched her chest. "Me? You think I'm the thief? Not me. We found the metal. We've been watching for two nights from the river."

He nodded, as though maybe he believed her.

"How about you, Mr. Willis?" Paul asked. "How come you're here?"

"G-garden," the man said.

"Garden? You can't grow nothing on the riverbank," Robbie said. "It's all muck."

Mr. Willis shook his head. "G-garden," he repeated.

Charlotte frowned, trying to understand. "Were you *guarding*? Keeping watch on the metal? Did you see it and decide to wait for the thief too? That's what we were doing."

Mr. Willis nodded. "Guarding. W-waiting for the thief. Th-three nights."

"Well, you caught me," Joseph Stankowski said.

His voice sounded so tired, so sad, it made Charlotte want to cry. What was it Paul had said a while back? That their thief was desperate. And not *mean* desperate, but poor. Flat-out broke.

Charlotte's cheeks were wet, even if she hadn't let go and cried. They were still standing out in the rain, and she was shivering. "Come on. Let's go to our house. We'll untangle this mess where it's dry."

Robbie stood with his feet planted. He crossed his arms and glared. "I don't want them coming to our house."

"Hush, Robbie," Charlotte said. She gathered her belongings and stepped closer to the rowboat. "We don't know the whole story yet."

"We know they took the metal. That means they're crooks. We don't need crooks at our house."

"Robert Michael Campbell, you hush. You're talking about a little girl. A boy you go to school with—" Charlotte's words got stuck in her throat. She saw Paul Rossi staring at her through the rain and she knew she had to say more.

She lifted her head and met Paul's eyes. "I . . . I did that too, Robbie. I accused somebody without knowing enough. I did it and I was wrong and I'm sorry. I know better now."

Paul ducked his head, then gave her a small smile.

"I heard what he said," Tommy Stankowski interrupted. "And I won't set foot in his darn house."

"You will if I tell you to," Joseph said. He hadn't raised his voice, but Charlotte heard steel in the quiet words.

"Would you come with us, Mr. Willis? We could use your help," Paul said.

"I-I c-can row." He stepped toward Joseph.

"You'll row my boat for me?" Joseph glanced down at his brother and sister. "All right, let's get us out of the rain."

Paul helped Charlotte and Robbie into his boat.

"You watch them good, Mr. Willis," Robbie shouted as he climbed aboard.

"Yep," Mr. Willis called. He followed the Stankowski kids along the bank to where they'd tied up their boat.

Paul gave his rowboat a shove and clambered in, then slid the loose oar into its oarlock.

"You're the one who needs watching," Charlotte told her brother. "No more nasty talk. At least not until we've heard what Joseph has to say."

Paul rowed across the current to the middle of the river and steered the boat so it was heading downstream. He held the oars out, steadying the boat against the current. "Thought we better row both boats down together. Is that all right?"

"Sure," Charlotte said. She could feel the current pushing against the bottom of the boat. "So they find the house."

"So they don't escape," Robbie said.

Charlotte knew that if she shined her flashlight on Robbie's face he'd be glaring. Well, tough. She watched upstream, and the Stankowskis' boat appeared. Mr. Willis was rowing. Joseph sat on a bench with the little girl. She was so small, six or seven at the most. Tommy perched in the bow, looking as stiff and stubborn as Robbie.

The river kept shoving them, the current strong and insistent. Paul pulled on the oars to steer and let the Mon carry them downstream toward home.

"Turn on the flashlight, Charlie," Robbie said.

"Good idea. Then they can see to follow us." She fumbled for the light.

"Give it to me," Robbie demanded, reaching across her lap. "I'm going to shine it on them, so they don't try to pull nothin'."

"You are the most mule-headed boy on the Monongahela." Charlotte tightened her grip on the flashlight.

Robbie grabbed an end of it and tugged hard.

"Hey, you two, quit rocking the boat," Paul warned.

Robbie didn't listen. He gave another hard yank and the boat lurched. Robbie tumbled over the side and into the fast-moving river.

CHAPTER 13
ALL WET

R obbie!" Charlotte screamed. Her thoughts raced every which way. It was just like the dream, her brother falling overboard. No. She shook her head. It couldn't be the dream. The wrong brother had fallen in the water.

"Charlotte!"

Paul's shout cleared her mind in an instant. This was no dream. She had one very real brother thrashing around in the deepest part of the Monongahela River.

"Go after him," Paul urged. "I'll keep the boat right with you."

"Me? In the river? How can I?" She didn't know if she'd spoken aloud. But of course she had to go after him. She kicked off her boots and wrestled free of the oilskin.

"Slide in. Don't jump or I'll capsize," Paul warned. "Go easy now."

Easy? Charlotte slipped her legs over the side. Icy water

sucked on her feet. Robbie was wearing shoes and a thick
oilskin. He'd never be able to swim with all that on. She let
herself slide in and cold smacked her in the chest. The river
drew her head under and she got a mouthful. That familiar
taste—mud and oil. Her clothes felt as heavy as pig iron.
She struggled to the surface, shook her head and spit.

Paul had somehow reached the flashlight and was
shining it on the river, dancing lights on muddy blackness.
"There," he called. "Behind us. Toward the middle." He
shined the light on a frothy, splashing place.

Fighting the current and the dead weight of her clothes,
Charlotte churned upstream. A clumsy stroke, then
another and another. The river pushed and she pushed
back, swimming in a ragged line toward Robbie.

At last she reached him and grabbed an arm. "Robbie?"

He coughed and twisted, towing her under the surface.

She fought her way upward and pulled him along,
spitting and coughing out water. Then there were arms
reaching for them. Boats on either side, oars to grab.
A grunt, and someone released the burden of Robbie's
weight from her arms. Then a strong arm hoisted her
upward, shoved her into Paul's boat.

Sprawled on the bottom, she heard voices. Coughing.
"Are you all right?"

"Charlie?" More coughs.

She pulled up into a sitting position in the bottom of
the boat, leaned against the seat. She was breathing hard,

and so cold. She tried to wipe the water from her face, but more streamed down from her hair.

The boat rocked. Under the bottom boards, she could feel the water, angry and roiling. Someone threw a heavy covering over her shoulders, and the boat turned, catching the current.

"Charlotte. Are you all right?" Paul's voice.

"I—I think so. Where's Robbie?"

"Other boat. He's okay. I'll get you home as fast as I can."

"Yes. Thanks." She let her eyes drift shut. Let the boat and Paul and the river do what they would. All she could think about was Robbie. He was safe.

That dream. She'd gotten it all wrong. She started to explain to Paul but her voice came out crooked and she was crying. More water, as if she needed more on a night like this.

By the time they climbed out of the rowboat, she'd caught her breath and stopped crying, but she couldn't seem to stop shivering. Paul took an arm to hold her steady as they made their way to her house. She glanced over her shoulder. Mr. Willis was half-carrying Robbie. Joseph marched at the end of their bedraggled parade, towing his brother and sister.

At the back door, Charlotte had to untangle herself
enough to reach for her key, still hanging on a soggy
string around her neck. At least that hadn't fallen off. But
even if it had, they would have been fine—didn't they have
a family of thieves coming home with them? She bit back
a giddy laugh.

After a quick scrub of her hands and face, and a
whole new set of clothes, Charlotte headed downstairs to
the kitchen, toweling her hair. She was the last to arrive.
Robbie had also changed, wrapping himself into his
warmest sweater. The rest had peeled off wet outer clothing. Damp towels and gear lay piled on the counter.
Everybody had gathered around the kitchen table.

Robbie and Mr. Willis were handing out plates of
scrambled eggs. "Missy?" he asked. "Y-you hurt?"

"No. Just cold."

Paul was passing out cups of hot chocolate. She
couldn't wait to wrap her hands around one.

Nothing had ever smelled quite so warm or wonderful.
She sipped, and it tasted sweet. And Mr. Willis had made
the best eggs. The table was silent as people ate and drank.
She wasn't the only cold and hungry person tonight. Just
the wettest. Her thick hair wouldn't dry till morning.

Somehow, she found her voice. "Thank you, whoever
pulled us out. Are you okay, Robbie? You didn't hurt yourself, did you?"

"Nah, I'm okay. That Joseph, he hauled me in." Robbie

had the grace to look apologetic. He turned. "Thanks."

"Hey. I got a brother. And a sister." He looked at Charlotte. "Are you really all right, or should we leave and come back tomorrow? You look like you could use a good night's sleep."

Charlotte shot a warning look toward Robbie. If he said another word about them running away, she'd pound him. But he didn't. "I'm fine. Just wet. Besides, I'll never sleep if you go home now. What's going on, Joseph? Are you a thief? How come you took our scrap?"

Joseph sat straight, with his hands flat against the kitchen table. "Like I said, I got a brother and a sister—"

"I helped," Tommy interrupted.

"Hush now, Tom," Joseph said.

Tommy didn't listen. "I did too help. I stuck gum in that lock so we could bust it open the second time. If you're sending him to jail, you gotta send me too." He folded his arms across his chest and tried to look ferocious.

To Charlotte's eye, he looked closer to tears. "Nobody's talking about jail just yet," she said. "Let your brother finish talking."

Joseph ducked his head as if to say thanks. "I ain't saying what we did was right or nothin'. But I had to do something. Kids got to eat." Joseph's cheeks were red, but

his eyes had dark shadows underneath that made him look
like he was sick with a fever.

"How'd you carry all that stuff?" Robbie demanded.
"Why'd you dump it by the river?"

"I boosted a truck," Joseph said. "But I didn't want to
use up too much gas and make somebody suspicious. So I
dumped the scrap upriver, and figured I'd collect it at
night in my boat."

"Wow, he stole a truck too," Robbie said.

"Borrowed, not stole." Tommy said. "He put the truck
back."

Joseph threw an arm around Tommy. "I'll do the talking now."

Charlotte couldn't help staring at Joseph. He was a
medium-sized guy, and bony. His cheeks and jaw looked
hard. In the light of the kitchen, she could see that his
hair wasn't black, just a dark brown.

"How about your folks? Can't they take care of things?"
Paul asked.

"They're gone."

The little girl sniffed. Joseph threw his other arm
around her. "It's all right, Tessa. I promised Ma, remember?"

She nodded and curled into his side. Tommy looked
at his lap.

"It's a long story," Joseph continued. "Our pa left back
in the thirties. Tessa was still a baby. He went to find
work. Never came back. We don't even know if he's alive."

"And your ma?" Charlotte asked.

"She died. She'd been real sick, and we was keeping care of her. But her lungs just gave out. It was cold and damp where we was staying. But even if she'd been in the hospital, she was so sick . . ."

Charlotte squeezed her eyes shut. If Pa left, or if something happened to Ma, what would she and Robbie do?

"You ain't the only one whose pa left." Paul spoke so softly Charlotte wasn't sure she'd heard the words right. "Mine went for work too, but he never found it. Found the wrong end of somebody's knife instead. At least my ma don't have to worry. She knows the truth."

"I didn't know . . ." Charlotte began. Poor Paul. No wonder he wanted to be a cop.

Paul shook his head. He turned back to Joseph. "With your folks gone, then, you've been taking care of these two?"

"Yep."

A thousand questions leapt into Charlotte's mind. How could he manage? How long had he been doing that? Did he have a job? Where did they live? Did anybody know? How did they get clothes? Food?

Paul's voice cut into her thoughts. "It's what my brothers would do."

"It's what our Jim would do too." Robbie's voice sounded like an echo.

Jim. That's who Charlotte had thought of when she'd first seen this Joseph Stankowski. And Robbie was right.

Jim would do whatever he could to keep them safe. So this man—this boy—in their kitchen wasn't mostly a thief. He was mostly a brother.

"When . . . when did your mother die?" she asked. "How long have you been taking care of everything?"

"About six months ago Ma got too sick to work anymore. We had to move then. Couldn't pay rent. I found us a shack down near the Rankin Bridge. Ain't much, but it keeps the worst of the weather out. She died a few weeks back. End of April."

"What did you do then?" Paul asked.

"Kept going, best we could. I fish some. The sisters at the convent help out with used clothes for the kids. They been doing that for a long while. I chop wood to keep a fire going. Work odd jobs when I can."

Paul shook his head. "No. I mean, what did you do about your mother? When she died?"

Charlotte rubbed at a scratch on the kitchen table. She didn't want to hear any more about dead mothers.

"We took her to church," Joseph said. He pulled his brother and sister closer to him. "Once we knew she was gone, we said our good-byes. Prayed over her. Then I tucked a blanket around her and wrapped her rosary around her hand. So they'd know she was a good Catholic. And we took her down to the Polish church in Pittsburgh."

"The woman on the church steps," Paul whispered. "St. Stanislas. Wow."

"Why?" The questions popped out before Charlotte could stop them. "Why didn't you tell the sisters at the convent and have the funeral here? We've got plenty of churches."

Joseph shook his head at her. "Don't you see? I couldn't tell the sisters. If I told, they'd take Tommy and Tessa away. Put them in an orphanage. Split up the family."

Tommy spoke again. He sat straight and stared right at Robbie. "Joey didn't tell nobody. And you can't neither. Me and Tessa, we ain't going to no orphanage."

"I—I wouldn't tell," Robbie said. "I promise. Cross my heart. But I do have a question. How come you didn't get the scrap last night? We heard you on the river."

"We weren't on the river last night," Joseph said. "Tessa had a stomachache."

"But I heard you," Robbie insisted. "There was a guy and he was yelling at a kid. Sounded just like you and Tommy. Tell him, Charlotte. You heard it too."

"We did," Charlotte said. "And we heard other people tonight, before you came. They sounded so close, but we didn't see any boats. It was spooky."

Joseph nodded. "Whisper Bend."

"What?" Paul asked.

"Whisper Bend. That's the name the river people give to the place where I stashed the scrap. There's something special about the limestone cliffs and the hill across the way. Makes sounds carry a long distance. When I was little, my pa had a pal stand way back on the top of the hill and sing old country songs in a real soft voice. Then Pa took me out in his boat. At Whisper Bend we could hear every word the guy sang. We could even hear when he stopped to cough and clear his throat."

"Whisper Bend," Charlotte repeated. She wondered if her pa knew about it. Wouldn't he be surprised if she could tell him something new about the river?

While Joseph talked, Mr. Willis had been leaning back next to the stove, watching. Now he stepped closer to the table and pointed to Tessa.

"L-little missy. Going to s-sleep."

He was right. She'd nodded off.

"Put her on the sofa in the living room, Joseph," Charlotte said. "I'll get a blanket."

It felt so good to move away from the table, away from the ugly facts Joseph had told. Charlotte climbed the steps to her room and pulled a quilt off her bed. Bending, she picked up a small soft doll and carried them both downstairs.

Joseph tucked his sister in, careful as any mother, and kissed her forehead. He was a good brother all right. He was Tessa's Jim. Charlotte glanced toward the front window, to Jim's star. She took a few steps and reached out to touch the points and whisper his name.

As she did, familiar footsteps sounded on the sidewalk. It was only ten-thirty, not nearly time for the shift change at the mill, but Ma was home. Charlotte heard more footsteps, then the kitchen door opening and shutting. She turned.

Ma strode into the living room, sooty and smudged. "Charlotte! Robbie! Who are these people? What in thunderation is going on?"

CHAPTER 14
EXTREME HARDSHIP

Nobody spoke at first. Charlotte and Robbie knew better. Ma didn't use strong language much, so when she came out with a *thunderation,* a person needed to watch out.

"Mrs. Campbell," Paul began. "We've been out on the river. We found the stolen metal and—"

Everyone else joined in, and even Charlotte couldn't make sense of the noise.

Ma held up her hands. "Quiet! First I just want to know, is anybody hurt? In danger?"

"No. We're just trying to figure out what happened," Charlotte said. "How come you're home so early, Ma?"

"I'll answer your questions after you've answered mine, thank you. But first, I'm going to get out of these filthy overalls. Don't anybody go anywhere." She marched upstairs.

Nobody else moved.

"She'll skin us alive," Robbie said. "I wish Pa were home."

"Don't worry," Charlotte grumbled. "We'll have to go through it all over again when he gets here."

"I'm sorry. It's my fault. We shouldn't have come back here," Paul said. "But my house—"

Charlotte shook her head at him. "Ma's mad now. Imagine if she'd come home and found nobody here. That would be a hundred times worse."

When Ma arrived with a clean face and wearing fresh clothes, they all marched back into the kitchen. Charlotte introduced everybody, then started to explain what had happened. People interrupted to tell their parts, and Ma had a bunch of questions. By the time Joseph had told about his mother dying, Charlotte knew Ma was finished being mad. Her eyes had filled up.

"You poor children," Ma said. "Whatever are you going to do?"

Tommy stuck out his chin again. "We ain't going to no orphanage. We'll run off to California first."

Tommy made Charlotte want to smile. He and Robbie were so much alike.

"Hush, Tommy," Joseph said. "I've been trying to figure that out, ma'am. I ain't afraid of work. And Tommy, he's all set to help at the grocery store, stacking food on the shelves this summer. That and what I can pick up doing odd jobs—"

"Odd jobs?" Ma asked. "I don't understand. There are jobs going begging all up and down the river. Why not get a real job with good pay?"

You had to give it to Ma, Charlotte thought. Her temper might get steamed up, but she could untangle troubles like nobody else.

Joseph shook his head. "I would if I could. But I turned eighteen back in the winter, when Ma was real sick. I had to kinda hide out, or Uncle Sam would come after me."

"The draft board." Ma's eyes narrowed. "Did you register?"

Joseph stared down at his feet. "No, ma'am. I know this is going to sound like I'm a slacker. And I know you've got a boy over there. Saw the blue star in your window. I'd go and do my bit if I could. Shoot, I wanted to enlist. But with Ma sick and the little ones . . ."

"Oh, what a mess." Ma ran her hand through her dark hair. "If you get a job, the draft board finds you. But if you don't work, how will you take care of your family?"

This was getting worse by the minute. What would Charlotte do in such a terrible situation? Or Jim, for that matter? What could anybody do?

"Yes, ma'am. That's why I took . . . stole the metal. There's a junk man down in Hazelwood. He don't ask too many questions. Pays in cash. I was planning to take the scrap down to him in my boat."

"M-m-mister. B-b-butler," Wagon Willie said. Every-one turned to look at him. It was the first he'd spoken since Ma had come home.

"Pardon me, Mr. Willis? What did you say?" Ma looked at him kindly.

"D-d-draft board."

Charlotte frowned. What was he talking about?

Ma shook her head. "I don't understand."

Mr. Willis took a deep breath. "H-h-hardship."

"Do you mean Mr. David Butler?" Ma's head snapped up and her eyes went wide. "He's head of the draft board, isn't he? Oh, Mr. Willis." Ma stood and reached out to shake Mr. Willis's hand. "I think you may have saved this poor boy."

"What?" "Who?" "How?" The table came alive with questions. Charlotte didn't know all the answers yet, but she recognized the look on Ma's face. It was the one she got when she was about to turn the whole house upside down for spring cleaning, and anybody who got in her way had better look out.

"Mrs. Campbell?" Joseph looked at her with serious brown eyes.

"What I think Mr. Willis is trying to tell us is this," Ma said. "We need to speak to Mr. Butler. The draft board has choices in situations like this one. There's a classification—extreme hardship, I believe it's called. Is that what you meant, Mr. Willis?"

The man nodded and smiled at Ma. "B-butler. I-I cut his g-grass."

She returned his smile. "You know Mr. Butler? Would you be willing to go with me and see Mr. Butler on this boy's behalf?"

Mr. Willis nodded again.

"But what would you say?" Joseph asked. "I ain't the kids' pa, I'm just their brother."

Charlotte shook her head. "You're the only pa they've got. And the Army isn't drafting fathers for the war. Won't that count for something?"

"Indeed it will," Ma said. "That's what I meant when I said it was a hardship case."

"And if they don't draft you, you can get a real job." Charlotte smiled. This could work. She went on. "If you had a real job, you'd make money, and they wouldn't have to send your brother and sister to an orphanage."

"But, Charlie, what about the metal?" Robbie said.

"We won't tell who took the metal. We'll just say we found it. Then we can haul it to the scrap yard," Charlotte said. "The whole town doesn't need to know the rest. We found it, so we can decide. But I would like to tell Mrs. Alexander and the principal. And Betsy."

She looked around the table. Robbie was nodding. So were Ma and Mr. Willis. Joseph and his brother Tommy had soft looks on their faces, like maybe they had a chance.

Paul was the only one not smiling. "I'm still worried.

What if the draft board is strict? What if they want to punish Joseph for not registering right away? If he goes to the draft board without enough strong arguments, they might say no."

"But it *is* a hardship case," Ma said. "Surely the draft board will see that."

Charlotte sighed. "If he already had a job and a house, he'd look like more of a real pa."

"You don't ask for much, do you, Charlotte," Paul said.

"I don't know. Charlotte's right." Joseph sounded worried. "If I don't go in strong to the draft board, I'd better not go in at all."

Charlotte jumped up. "If he could get a *war* job, the draft board would excuse him from the Army, wouldn't they? What's that called, Ma?"

"It's called a deferment. Men get them for working at defense jobs in vital industries. Of course—I could recommend you at the mill! We're shorthanded. We had a breakdown on the line tonight, and they've had to shut down production until it gets fixed. With not enough people, maintenance is tough. And they're building a new furnace, so they're looking for strong young men. They'd take you on in a minute."

Charlotte felt a huge weight lift off her shoulders. If the draft board treated Joseph like a father to his brother and sister, *and* he had a war job . . . She smiled at him, but he'd turned pale.

"In the mill?" He took a deep breath. "Sure, I'll give it a try . . ." His Adam's apple bobbed as he swallowed a couple of times.

"What?" Charlotte asked. "What's the matter?"

Joseph looked ashamed. "I'll do it. I'll do whatever it takes. But I'm a river rat. They got a concrete fence around the mill and barbed wire, like a prison. And all that fire— when I look at the mill at night, I think that's what the priest must be talking about when he warns about the fires of hell." Joseph shuddered.

Charlotte understood exactly how he felt. She felt like that every time Pa made her help on the boat. The boat! "You're a river rat. How about working on a tug? Pa's short-handed. And it's defense work."

"Would he hire me?"

"I'm sure he would," Ma said.

Charlotte knew from the look on Ma's face that if Pa had his doubts, Ma would convince him. But Pa wouldn't need much convincing. Hadn't he said they all needed to hold on to each other to get through the hard times? If this wasn't a hard time, what was?

Even Paul was beginning to look happier. "Now all we have to do is find him a place to live. Shoot, it's too late . . ." He paused. "See, my ma rents our top floor to some girls who came up from West Virginia to work in the mill. That's why we couldn't go there tonight—I'm not supposed to make a racket or bother them. If only

Ma could kick them out. But she can't."

"Maybe the job will be enough for the draft board," Joseph said. "If you mean it."

"Of course we do," Ma said. "If there were just a place for you to stay, and someone to care for the children while you're working. But so many women are working full shifts in the factories and mills . . ."

"I know!" Robbie said. He pounded the table and grinned. "I got it. It's perfect. You can stay with Mrs. Dubner."

Charlotte's mouth fell open. "Robbie, you're nuts! Mrs. Dubner's crazy. And all those cats."

"Only three," he said.

"You mean three hundred," she laughed.

Robbie sighed. "She feeds all the strays, but only three live there. Two gray ones and a stripey kitten. And she's not crazy, Charlie. She's just lonely."

Ma turned to him, a serious look on her face. "What do you mean, Robbie?"

He shrugged. "Well, with her boys gone, she hasn't had anybody. And she's real nice. Bakes good ginger cookies."

Charlotte could not believe her brother had been spending time with old Mrs. Dubner. Was he turning crazy too?

Ma looked stern. "Robert Michael Campbell, how do you know all this?"

"Aw, Ma, I didn't have anything to do after I hurt my

hand—you wouldn't let me collect scrap. So I went to see her. She gave me cookies and let me pet her cats. She's got lots of room with just her living there."

"Wait a minute," Charlotte interrupted, as the rest of Robbie's words finally hit her. "What boys? Does she really have kids?"

"Not anymore." Robbie shook his head and sighed again. "They both died. Long time ago. They got gassed in what she calls the Great War. But she's got beds and stuff. It's lots better than a shack. And I bet if you gave her some money, she'd cook for you too."

Ma looked around the table. "I don't know about the rest of you, but it sounds to me like things may work out." Ma checked her watch. "It's awfully late. I'd say we have plenty to keep us busy tomorrow. Joseph, will you and your family stay here tonight? We've got a room free on the third floor."

"Yes, ma'am. And thank you. Thank you all. Getting caught might have been the best thing that's happened to us in a while." With that he stood and picked up Tessa to carry her upstairs.

Ma shook hands with Mr. Willis. "Thank you so much. Shall we meet with the principal tomorrow and then arrange things with Mr. Butler?"

Mr. Willis nodded and smiled. Paul stepped toward the door and grinned at Charlotte. He stuck out his hand. "Shake?"

"Shake. We did a great job. Wait till we tell Betsy tomorrow. Wait till she finds out all she missed."

He waved and followed Mr. Willis back out into the rainy night.

Ma turned to Charlotte. "Now, young lady, will you tell me why I found two sets of soggy clothes in the bathtub? And why your hair looks like a rat's nest? You seem to have left out that part."

In all the excitement, Charlotte had actually forgotten. "I . . . Robbie . . . We . . . Well, he fell in the river, and I went in after him."

"*You?* You went in the water?"

"I had to, Ma. Paul was steering the boat. I guess I'm part river rat too."

Ma pulled Charlotte into her arms and held her tight. "I should scold you for being out there in the first place, but somehow, I haven't the heart. That was a brave thing to do, sweetheart. Your pa and I—I can't tell you . . . With Jim gone, if you or Robbie—"

"It's okay, Ma. Really. Robbie and I are swell. And there's something else." Charlotte took Ma's hand and tugged her toward the front window. She reached up and touched the points of Jim's star. "Jim's going to come home safe. I just know he is."

"Because?"

"Because he's as bad as Robbie. Worse maybe."

"What are you talking about, Charlotte?"

"Jim's nosy. He can't stand it if somebody knows something that he doesn't." Charlotte's fingers itched for paper and a pencil. "I've got a plan, Ma. I'll write a letter and tell him a little about tonight. But I'll leave out all the good parts. I'll pretend it's because of the censors. But then Jim will *have* to come home so he can find out what we've been up to. I'm sure of it."

"Ah, Charlotte," Ma said. She hugged her again. "What will you cook up next, girl?"

"Please, Ma, don't!" Robbie raced in. "Don't let her cook any more potatoes. She always burns them." He made a face.

"Oh you, buster. You'll eat what I cook and you'll like it." Charlotte messed up his damp hair with both her hands.

Brothers, she thought. Brothers.

1942

A Peek into the Past

Looking Back: 1942

In the spring of 1942, the world was at war. German troops had taken over nearly all of Europe, and Japan had conquered most of Asia. But wartime was still new to Americans. The United States had entered the war only a few months earlier. Many families, like Charlotte's, had sent sons or brothers to fight.

On April 28, 1942, the day Charlotte's story opens, President Franklin D. Roosevelt spoke to the nation in one of his frequent radio talks, called "fireside chats." He admitted the war was going badly for the United States, and he asked ordinary Americans at home to sacrifice for victory, just as their fighting men were doing overseas. Like Charlotte, adults and children everywhere quickly found new ways to pitch in and help their country win the war.

President Roosevelt's radio speeches inspired the nation during World War II.

The president's message had special meaning in steel-producing towns. To win the war, America needed ships and weapons—which required steel, and lots of it. During the war, western Pennsylvania river towns blazed night and day. Smoke and soot from tall chimneys filled the skies, slag heaps smoldered, tugs and barges clogged the rivers. Mills like the Edgar Thomson added new furnaces so they could pour endless tons of steel. In fact, the Pittsburgh area, including Braddock, poured nearly 30 percent of all the steel used by America and her allies during World War II. This amazing effort earned the area a new name—*Victory Valley*.

All over the country, schools, scout troops, and church groups held scrap drives, collecting metal to be recycled. They gathered items made of aluminum, tin, copper, iron, and steel, sorted them, and sent them to factories to be melted down. Eventually, so much metal was turned into war supplies that there wasn't even enough to make diaper pins! People also collected and

Above: A steel mill at night.
At right: A proud scrapper

Standing on a scrap pile, these schoolchildren are all making the "V for Victory" sign.

recycled paper, rubber, and even lard, which was used in making artillery shells and grenades.

Americans pitched in to be sure their soldiers and allies also got the tons of food, clothing, and other supplies they needed. Families planted backyard "Victory gardens" so more

farm products could go to soldiers. Schools in farm areas closed in spring and fall so students could help plant and harvest crops. And everyone saved money to buy war bonds and stamps to help the government pay for all the needed supplies.

The United States shipped so many goods overseas that serious shortages occurred at home. Sugar, fruit, meat, rubber, metal, paper, clothing, leather, and gasoline all grew scarce. The government began *rationing*, or limiting, how much of these products each family could buy. Imagine having to make one pair of shoes last a whole year, or saving sugar coupons for weeks to bake holiday cookies!

The government issued ration coupons to each household. People couldn't buy scarce products like sugar or gas without them.

With so many men overseas, workers were in short supply, too. Women like Charlotte's mother, who had worked at home caring for their families, took factory jobs. They traded dresses for overalls and made steel, ships, bombs, bullets, and thousands of airplanes. Their work was vital to America's war effort. And 350,000 women joined the military, handling non-combat jobs such as nursing, office work, packing parachutes, and testing new airplanes, so that men could fight.

Millions of women took jobs making war supplies.

As Americans at home did their part for the war, a sense of unity and shared purpose took hold across the country. People grew strong and determined. But they were often afraid, too. Air-raid drills frightened many children. As sirens blared, people in homes and schools darkened their windows and

Many families made a special shelter in the basement, where they hid during air-raid drills.

hid in basements, practicing what to do if warplanes attacked. Children in industrial areas knew that their towns were likely bombing targets if German warplanes crossed the Atlantic.

Radios and newspapers reported battles lost, islands over-run, and ships sunk. Movie theaters ran vivid newsreels before every featured film. Up on the movie screen, children saw battle scenes, German soldiers, and Japanese warplanes. Such images were especially chilling to people with loved ones fighting in the war.

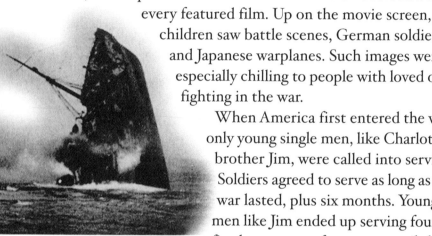

When America first entered the war, only young single men, like Charlotte's brother Jim, were called into service. Soldiers agreed to serve as long as the war lasted, plus six months. Young men like Jim ended up serving four or five long years—from 1941 until the war ended in 1945, or even longer.

Theaters showed newsreels about the war, including scenes of battles and sinking ships.

Mothers hung a blue star in the window for each son in service, as Charlotte's mother did. If a son was killed, a gold star replaced the blue one. Some families had more than one gold star before the war was over.

Eventually, married men and fathers also had to serve in the military. Only men with medical problems, extreme family hard-ships, or jobs vital to the war—like the work Charlotte's father did—were *deferred*, or excused, from service.

Lonely soldiers cherished letters from home.

When a man served in the war, his family did not know where he was or how much danger he was facing. The government *censored* all letters to and from servicemen, cutting out words that might tell enemy spies about troop movements or war production. Letters between soldiers and their families show the heartbreak and sadness these separations caused, and also the bravery of women at home, who wrote strong, encouraging letters to their men overseas. One such woman signed each letter "all my love, all my life."

Millions of American men and women served in the war. Many did not return—400,000 Americans died in World War II, and nearly 17 million people died across the world.

In the steel towns of Pennsylvania, as in the rest of the country, World War II required patriotism and sacrifice. Americans turned all their efforts to victory, believing with President Roosevelt that freedom must be preserved, whatever the cost.

GEOGRAPHICAL NOTE

There really is a Whisper Bend on the Monongahela River, but for purposes of this story, the cove has been moved several miles downstream to the town of Braddock, and a lock and dam have been moved upstream.

About the Author

Katherine Ayres loved hearing stories and making them up even before she could read and write. She did part of her growing up near the beach in Long Island, New York, where she enjoyed the water all year round and especially in summer. Now that she lives in Pittsburgh, many trips take her near one of the city's three rivers, where she can watch tugboats pushing heavy barges. As she prepared to write this book she spent a day on a tug and observed the muddy Monongahela up close. Studying history and learning about interesting places is one of the best parts of writing books, says Ms. Ayers. She's also written two books that take place in Ohio (where she was born), *Family Tree* and *North by Night.*